Zoey 101™

Dra… …a

Adapted by Jan… …a Hines Stephens

Based on "Defending Dustin" written by
Anthony Del Broccolo and
"The Play" written by Steven Molaro

Based on *Zoey 101* created by Dan Schneider

SCHOLASTIC INC.

New York Toronto London Auckland Sydney
Mexico City New Delhi Hong Kong Buenos Aires

ISBN 0-439-80177-X

12 11 10 9 8 7 6 5 4 3 6 7 8 9 10/0

Printed in the U.S.A.

First printing, November 2005

Bully Trouble

Zoey Brooks walked quickly across the Pacific Coast Academy campus, flanked by her roommates, Nicole Bristow and Dana Cruz. This was actually a big deal, because for the first two weeks of school Nicole and Dana pretty much just screamed at each other. But since they'd worked things out — with a little help from Zoey — everything was cool. Now all they had to worry about was the usual boarding school stuff, like getting their homework done and staying on their teachers' good sides . . . which, for one thing, meant getting to class on time.

"Hey, will you guys slow down?" Nicole complained.

"We're going to be late for class," Zoey said, barely slowing down.

Nicole knew that, of course. She was generally very prompt. But it was pretty warm out, and she could feel herself getting a little . . . damp. And that meant her hair could frizz. And frizzy hair was her absolute arch-enemy. So she had to slow down.

"Better late than sweaty," she said.

Zoey and Dana stopped in their tracks. "She has a point," Zoey said with a nod. She stepped forward again, moving more slowly. Sweaty was not pleasant . . . for anyone. And if Nicole's hair started to frizz, she and Dana would hear about it for the rest of the day. Zoey was glad she didn't have to worry about frizz. She spent little time on her shoulder-length blond hair in the morning — choosing between braids, a ponytail, a ponytail with a twist, or down straight. Then she could get on with what to wear. Today she'd chosen sneakers, jean shorts with a retro belt, and a printed tee.

Now that they had slowed down, Zoey had a chance to take in the morning. It was another beautiful day at PCA — clear blue sky, slight breeze, and the sound of Pacific Ocean waves in the background. Zoey grinned. She still had a hard time believing that she went to school in such a gorgeous place.

"Oooh!" Nicole said suddenly. "Cute boy to the left. Green shirt, backpack." Nicole couldn't believe how many cute boys went to her new school. Since this was the first year PCA had admitted girls, there were a lot more boys than girls on campus. And Nicole thought that was just fine — as long as she could keep her hair under control.

Zoey casually looked over at the guy — trying not to be obvious. She had to agree he was pretty cute, even if he looked like he knew it. He definitely knew the girls were checking him out. He flashed them a smile as he adjusted his backpack.

"How cute is he?" Nicole asked with a little squeal.

Dana eyed the guy casually. She liked boys fine, but she wasn't about to get all worked up over them. "Seven," she said casually.

"No, nine!" Nicole objected. Dana was way too critical, and not just about boys. She always had something negative to say. "He's a nine, right, Zoey?"

Zoey looked at the guy again. He was definitely in the hottie category — tall, short reddish hair, cute smile. But his clothes . . . "Yeah," she agreed. "But I gotta take off for the red shorts with the green shirt. He looks like Christmas."

Dana nodded, squinting at the colorful outfit as if it hurt her eyes. She generally stuck to black and gray. "Agreed."

Nicole looked a little put out. "I like Christmas," she pouted, with her hands on her hips.

The girls were on their way again when Dustin rushed up to them. "Whaddup, Zo'?" he greeted.

Zoey grinned at her little brother. They lived on different parts of the campus, so she didn't see him as much as she did when they were home. She actually kind of missed him. "Hey, kiddo."

"Where are you off to?" Zoey asked.

"Just goin' to geometry class," Dustin replied.

"Geometry?" Dana repeated. That was not part of the sixth-grade curriculum — even at PCA.

"In *sixth* grade?" Nicole wrinkled her nose in confusion.

Zoey beamed. "Yep. Dustin takes eighth-grade math 'cause he's brilliant," she explained with a shrug. Dustin was a great little brother and a math whiz.

"Awwww!" Nicole and Dana cooed. Obviously Zoey was proud — so sweet!

Dustin grimaced. "Zo-eeeey." He was glad she was proud of him and all, but did she have to go off like that in front of her friends? It was embarrassing! He had to get out of there — fast. "I gotta go," he said.

Zoey eyed her little brother's outfit. It needed some help. "Wait, lemme fix you." She started to untuck his maroon shirtsleeve button-down so his "Jamaica" T-shirt showed underneath.

"What are you doin'?" Dustin asked, a little annoyed. Sometimes Zoey acted like she was his mom — except that his mom would probably tuck his shirt *in*.

"Making you look cooler," Zoey said, pushing his socks down so they didn't meet his board shorts. Next she turned her attention to his mop of blond hair. "Oh, and your hair's too neat." She rumpled it as a couple of kids in Dustin's class passed by.

Dustin heard the sixth graders laugh, and scowled. "Will ya stop?" he protested. "I gotta get to class," he said. In a second he was gone.

"Don't let the eighth graders intimidate you!" Zoey called out.

Dustin turned back and gave her a lopsided grin. Was she serious? He could keep up with the eighth graders any day of the week. "C'mon! I fit right in!" he yelled back.

A few minutes later, Dustin sat in geometry class. Luckily his seat was in the front row — otherwise he might not have been able to see over the other kids' heads. Eighth graders were huge!

Dustin didn't mind that he was the smallest kid in the room. Good things came in small packages. Besides, he didn't have to wrestle these kids — just do math — and for him, math was a snap.

In the front of the room, Mr. Kirby was watching a student named Keith Finch scribble out numbers, trying to work out a problem on the chalkboard. Mr. Kirby waited patiently, holding an open textbook and watching the student grapple with the tricky problem.

"Okay," Keith said, shooting a cocky grin at the rest of the class, "the right answer is twenty-eight pi."

"Hmmmmm," Mr. Kirby said, eyeing Keith's work. "Class, are his calculations correct?"

Most of the students mumbled to themselves, or looked at the floor, or got busy searching for things in their backpack — they were clueless.

Dustin raised his hand. "Actually, he used the wrong formula," he pointed out.

The class started to murmur again, but this time they sounded surprised.

Keith glared at Dustin. "What are you talkin' about?" he growled.

Dustin got to his feet and walked to the front of the class. "I'll show ya," he said cheerfully, taking the chalk from the bigger boy. He turned to the board and got to work fixing Keith's problem. "The formula to find the area of a circle is πr^2, not $2\pi r$." He quickly scribbled several numbers and letters on the board. "So the right answer is 196π."

Dustin grinned at the class. They looked pretty impressed! So did Mr. Kirby. Keith, on the other hand . . .

Dustin was only as tall as Keith's crossed arms. Looking up slowly, past the black T-shirt with the lightning bolt on it, he met Keith's narrowed eyes. Keith looked mad. Really, really mad.

The sinking feeling in Dustin's stomach told him that he was in for it. "Just sayin' . . ." Dustin smiled sheepishly.

A bunch of the kids in the class snickered, and Keith looked like he was going to pummel Dustin right then and there.

"Very impressive, Dustin," Mr. Kirby said with a nod. Dustin wondered if being impressive could get him into the math-whiz protection program. He had a feeling he was going to need it. But before he could escape Keith and get back to his seat, the bell rang and kids started gathering up their stuff and heading for the door.

"Don't forget your homework, it's due tomorrow," Mr. Kirby reminded them as they filed out.

Dustin raced to his desk and threw his books into his bag. He could feel Keith's eyes on his back. Pulling his pack onto his back, he raced out of the classroom and down the hall. He had to get out of there!

Dustin burst out of the math building. He made it

through the quad and was racing through the maze of white tables outside the cafeteria when he finally dared to look over his shoulder. The coast was clear. Whew! But when Dustin turned back around, he ran right into Keith.

Panting, Dustin looked up at the huge eighth grader. He was done for. "Keith," he said, trying to sound casual. "Nice to see ya again."

"You think you're real smart, doncha?" he hissed.

Dustin gulped. Keith probably *could* snap him in two. Maybe he should try a little humor. . . . "Well, one time I did get a hundred and twelve on a spelling test. Funny story. See, I was —"

Without saying a word, Keith lifted Dustin off the ground. Dustin's gray skater sneakers dangled a full two feet off the ground.

"I notice you've lifted me," Dustin said, stating the obvious and trying to stay calm. His heart thudded in his chest.

Keith still didn't say anything. He didn't have to. His menacing look said it all. Finally he lowered Dustin to the ground. "All right, Dustin," he said, opening his backpack. "Since you're so smart, you're gonna do my math homework for me." He thrust his math textbook into Dustin's hands.

"But I —"

"And my history homework." Keith shoved another book at Dustin.

"But I don't think it's right for —"

"And my French homework." Keith added another book to the pile.

Dustin gasped. "But I don't know French," he protested feebly.

Keith leaned over and put his face right up to Dustin's. "Then you got a lotta work to do, doncha?" He smirked.

"Oui," Dustin squeaked. He had just used the only French word he knew.

"You have all my homework done by tomorrow morning, got it?" Keith ordered.

Dustin willed himself to be strong. "Um . . . what happens if I don't?" he asked.

Keith leaned in even closer. His nose almost touched Dustin's face, and, ew, Dustin could *smell* him. "B-a-d, b-a-d things," Keith said, narrowing his already beady eyes. Dustin got the point. Keith was not to be messed with.

Mama Zoey

Zoey popped in her earphones, picked a tune off her little white MP3 player, and prepared to let the music play. Classes were over for the day, and she was taking it easy on her way back to her dorm. The academics at PCA were intense, so whenever she had a minute or two of downtime, she took advantage of it.

All around her, other kids appeared to be doing the same. Kids rode bikes or skateboards, gabbed in groups, or just soaked up some sun.

"Hey, need a ride?" Zoey heard a voice say over her music. She quickly cut the tunes and smiled at her friend Chase. Chase was her first and best guy friend at PCA. He'd shown her around the campus the first day, helped her deal with her roommate crises the second week of school, and was generally a great guy.

"Hey," Zoey greeted him. Chase was wearing a

red motorcycle-style helmet and his curls stuck out at crazy angles. "You goin' by my dorm?"

Chase grinned. He'd give Zoey a ride to San Francisco if she wanted one — he thought she was that cool. "I am now."

Zoey hopped onto Chase's bike — standing on the pegs that jutted out from the back wheel.

Zoey grabbed ahold of his shoulders. "You sure this is safe?" she asked.

"That depends on your definition of safe," Chase admitted, taking off.

They rode across campus, dodging benches, tables, and students. Chase turned a corner and slowed to a halt next to a janitor wearing a navy uniform and a PCA baseball hat. He was pushing a cleaning cart.

"Hey, Herb!" Chase yelled.

"Chase!" Herb looked glad to see him. "How you doin', kid?"

"Great," Chase replied. "I'm just lovin' school. Except, y'know, the whole 'learning' part." He glanced toward Zoey. Whoops. He'd forgotten to introduce her. "Oh, this is Zoey," he said.

Zoey gave Herb a little wave. "Hi, Herb."

"Nice to meet ya, Zoey," Herb said in his New Jersey accent.

"Hey, did you get the part in that movie?" Chase asked. "Herb's an actor, you know," he explained to Zoey.

"Nice," Zoey said with a nod.

"Struggling actor," Herb said, waving it off. "And nah, I didn't get the part."

"Their loss," Chase said. "Herb's awesome. Watch." Turning back to Herb with a smile, Chase lifted his chin. "Do some Shakespeare."

Herb shook his head. "Oh, I dunno . . . I don't really like to —"

Zoey was about to tell Herb not to worry about it, she could see his acting another time — when he suddenly launched into a soliloquy, complete with a perfect British accent.

"For who would bear the whips and scorns of time, th' oppressor's wrong, the proud man's contumely . . ."

Zoey raised an eyebrow at Chase. "Contumely?" she whispered.

Chase shrugged. He had no clue what *contumely* meant.

". . . The pangs of despised love," Herb finished.

Chase and Zoey clapped. "Wow!" Zoey said. "Impressive."

"What's that mean?" Chase asked. Shakespeare

always sounded great, but he never understood what the heck they were talking about.

Herb shook his head. “I really got no idea,” he admitted as his walkie-talkie crackled to life.

“Hey, Herb,” the voice over the walkie said. “We got a one-fourteen in progress outside the cafeteria.”

“Yikes,” Herb said. Then, into the talkie, “Copy that. I’m on the move.”

“What’s a one-fourteen?” Zoey asked, curious. Herb obviously had a whole slew of codes for various janitorial issues.

“Vomit,” Herb said matter-of-factly. “See ya.” He pushed his cart up the path and launched into a new soliloquy. “For who doth mop the chunks of lunch spewed forth by the nauseous and the queasy. ’Tis the noble janitor’s plight. . . .”

Zoey was trying to get the barf image out of her head when Dustin ambled up.

“Hey, Zo’. Hi, Chase,” he said, biting into his Bing Bong snack cake. He was trying to drown his miseries with some creamy filling and sprinkles. It was helping . . . a little.

“S’up, little D?” Chase greeted.

Zoey looked disapprovingly at her little brother’s

sugary snack. "Dustin, you know you're not supposed to be eating junk like that!" she scolded. Dustin had a serious sugar habit, and Zoey was always trying to nip it in the bud. She grabbed the Bing Bong out of his hand.

Chase nodded in agreement. "She's right," he said, pulling the Bing Bong out of her hand. "You gotta dip this in chocolate syrup. Waaaay better."

Zoey's jaw dropped. What was Chase thinking? "Chase!" she griped, taking the snack cake back into possession.

"Just gimme back my Bing Bong," Dustin groused. There she went again — acting like a parent instead of a big sister. Zoey could be so . . . uncool.

"No." Zoey shook her head. Somebody had to look out for Dustin. If she didn't, he'd probably turn into a frosted snack cake. "Growing boys do not need to be eating Bing Bongs."

"Gah!" Dustin threw up his hands. She was driving him nuts! "Would ya quit actin' like Mom?" He pushed past her and walked down the path.

Zoey couldn't believe her ears. She was not acting like their mom! She was just trying to help Dustin. "Can you believe what he said?" she asked Chase. He'd back her up for sure — Chase always understood.

"Kinda." Chase shrugged.

"Excuse me?!" Zoey shot Chase a look. Where was her supportive friend?

"Well, you do kinda baby him sometimes," Chase said slowly. He didn't want to get into a fight.

Zoey whacked Chase on the arm. "I do not!" she protested.

Chase rubbed his shoulder sulkily through his blue button-down shirt. "Okay, that bruise should appear in about twenty minutes."

"I don't treat Dustin like a baby," Zoey pouted. It was her job to look after him, wasn't it? After all, he was her little brother and they were away from home.

Chase debated for half a second. Should he just agree with Zoey to avoid a fight? The thing was, he didn't agree with her. And the other thing was, they were friends. And friends told each other the truth. So he had to tell Zoey the truth. "You do," he repeated.

Zoey held up the Bing Bong, eyeing it like a criminal. "Why, because I won't let him eat garbage like this?" she asked.

"Garbage?!" Chase repeated incredulously, grabbing the snack cake. Zoey obviously had no appreciation for junk food whatsoever. What was wrong with her, anyway? Wasn't she a teenager? "You're talking about nature's perfect combination of chemicals and sugar."

Zoey rolled her eyes and crossed her arms over her printed top. She just didn't see the attraction of overly sweet, artificially colored snack foods. They tasted like cardboard. But Chase was obviously not going to be convinced. "I gotta go," she finally said.

Sighing heavily, Zoey strode away from Chase, leaving him holding the Bing Bong. Chase grinned and took a bite. But before he could even swallow, Zoey was back. She grabbed the Bing Bong out of his hand and held her own hand out, palm up in front of his face. Like a bad dog, Chase opened his mouth and let his partially chewed bite of chemical-and-sugar perfection fall into her hand.

Zoey tried not to wince as the disgusting glop of chewed snack cake landed on her hand. Then, shooting Chase a look, she turned on her heel and headed back to her dorm, dropping the offensive glop and cake it came from into the nearest trash can.

Late Night at PCA

Later that night, Dustin stared at his computer screen. He propped his head up with his hand, trying to stay focused. It was past one o'clock in the morning, and he was wiped out. But he still had tons of homework to do — Keith's homework.

Dustin glanced over at his unmade bed. It looked sooo comfy. If only he could lie down for a minute. The computer screen in front of him was becoming blurry. He needed to take a break.

As soon as he did, thoughts of Keith flashed through his mind. *You have all my homework done by tomorrow morning, got it? Or b-a-d, b-a-d things will happen. . . .*

Dustin jumped a little in his seat. Keith was a giant, a monster, an eighth-grade maniac! Who knew what he was capable of? With a huge sigh, Dustin reached over and poured himself a large cup of coffee. It was going to be a very long night.

Across campus, Dana, Nicole, and Zoey were all sound asleep in their beds. Then, out of the blue . . .

Bang! Bang! Bang!

Nicole bolted upright, totally confused. She'd been dreaming about a new hair product that guaranteed frizz-free hair. "What's happening?" she cried.

Dana threw the covers aside and climbed out of bed wearing a black dragon tee and black pajama shorts. Couldn't a girl get a decent night's sleep around here? "Who's bangin' on our door?!" she griped.

Zoey switched on the green lamp by her bed. "I dunno," she said.

Bang! Bang! Bang! The noise was getting louder and more desperate. Zoey jumped out of bed and opened the door. Chase and Michael tumbled into the room, totally freaked. And that wasn't all. Chase was holding a dog.

"Hey," Michael panted.

"What's up?" Chase added, out of breath but trying to sound casual. He didn't want to make a big deal out of their late-night visit.

Zoey stared at the two boys and dog standing in

front of her. "What are you doing here?" she asked. Did they have any idea what time it was?

"At one-thirty in the morning?" Dana added pointedly.

Chase thrust the dog at Zoey. "You gotta hide Elvis!"

Nicole was still sleepy . . . and confused. "Who's Elvis?" she asked.

"Our dog!" Michael whispered a little frantically. "You gotta hide our dog!"

Zoey held up her hands. "Wait. Slow down and tell us what's goin' on." She wasn't about to get snowballed into taking care of some four-legged creature . . . even if he was adorable with his little white face and brown ears.

"Well, we found this dog on the beach. . . ." Chase explained, talking fast. He kept looking at the door, too. Not a good sign.

"And he didn't have any tags," Michael went on.

". . . So we've been keeping him in our room."

"Doesn't PCA have a rule against pets?" Nicole asked, suddenly feeling wide-awake.

"Yes, they do," Chase admitted. "That's why we're here."

"See, our D.A. was in our room tonight and he smelled the dog," Michael lamented.

"D.A." Chase turned to Zoey. "Short for Dorm Advisor."

Zoey shot Chase a look. Did he think she'd arrived at PCA the day before? She'd been here for three whole weeks! "I know," she said flatly.

"OK. That's short for okay," Chase rambled.

Zoey held up her hands. "Stop it," she commanded. One-thirty A.M. was not a good time to get Chase on a ramble.

"Anyway, now our D.A.'s all suspicious." Michael continued the story.

"So you gotta hide him until things cool down." Chase was talking fast and looking back and forth between Zoey and her roomies. The short-haired dog in his arms was looking back and forth, too.

Nicole shook her head. "No."

"Will ya?" Michael begged. "Pleeeeeeaaaaaase?"

Chase grabbed Elvis's snout, smushing his cheeks together. "Look at this face," he said. Elvis whimpered.

Zoey was torn. Elvis was adorable, and she loved animals. How great would it be to have a dog? But it was totally, completely against the rules. "We can't keep a —"

Zoey was interrupted by Chase's cell phone. Chase handed Elvis to Michael, pulled the phone out of his pocket, and flipped it open. "Yeah?" he said. Then, a second later, "Aw, man! Be right there!" He snapped the phone closed and shoved it back in his pocket.

"Who was it?" Michael asked.

"Logan. D.A. did a room check. Now he's looking for us!"

Michael's brown eyes opened wide. "We gotta get back!" he cried.

Michael thrust Elvis into Zoey's arms. The two boys raced for the door.

"Wait! Guys!" Zoey called, trying to ignore Elvis's soft fur, sweet face, and the adorable brown spot on his back. "We can't keep this dog in our —"

Wham! The door slammed closed, leaving the three girls and Elvis alone in the room.

Zoey looked at Nicole, then Dana. "Looks like we have a new roommate," she said with a shrug.

"Oh, no, we don't," Dana said, crossing her arms across her chest and heading for the door.

"Where are you going?" Nicole asked, looking worried. The last thing she wanted was for Dana to turn poor Elvis in.

"To tell our D.A." She gave Elvis a scowl. He was

kind of cute, but he probably had doggy breath and would shed all over the place. "I don't want that mutt in my room." She opened the door.

Zoey crossed the room in a flash and closed the door. Dana could be a little sour, but Zoey was learning that underneath her tough exterior she was a nice person. Besides, Michael had handed Elvis to her, and she was going to do her best to keep him safe.

"Just for a little while, okay?" Zoey pleaded.

"C'mon," Nicole added, looking at Elvis's sweet little face. "If you turn him in, they'll take him to the pound."

Dana eyed her roommates — and Elvis. He gazed at her with his brown puppy eyes, looking hopeful. "Three days," Dana finally said. "That's it."

"Yay!" Nicole cheered, giving Elvis a scratch.

"Aw, did you hear that, Elvis?" Zoey asked, lifting his furry chin. She was trying to forget the fact that pets were against the rules. "You're our new roomie — yes, you are!"

"He's so cute!" Nicole crooned. "Wait." She held up a hand. "He is a he, right?"

Nicole and Zoey peeked quickly between Elvis's legs. "Yup." Nicole nodded vigorously. "He's a he."

Big Sister Act

Dustin stared down at the piles of papers and textbooks on the table in front of him. His hair was rumpled and his clothes looked slept in. But Dustin barely noticed. He was running out of time! Keith would find him any minute, and discover that he hadn't finished his homework, even though he'd stayed up almost all night.

B-a-d, b-a-d things . . . Keith's voice echoed in his head. Dustin shivered and got back to the math homework in front of him. He just wished the numbers would stop jumping around!

"Dustin?" He heard someone call his name . . . Zoey. Great, just what he needed — his sister showing up to tell him how to take care of himself.

"Oh. Hey, Zo'," Dustin greeted her. He was too tired to say much else.

"You look horrible," Zoey said, pulling out a chair and sitting down next to him. His hair was *too* messy, there were huge circles under his eyes, and he was wearing the same clothes he'd had on the day before.

"Yeah," Dustin replied. He may as well tell her what was going on. She would drag it out of him, anyway. "I was up until four in the morning."

Zoey's jaw dropped. "Why?"

"This mean guy named Keith Finch . . ."

"Yeah?" Zoey prodded.

"He's making me do all his homework," Dustin finished.

"What?!" Zoey bellowed, suddenly furious. Who did this Keith kid think he was? "He can't do that!"

"Yeah, he can," Dustin assured her. "He's huge. His head weighs more than I do."

"Did he threaten to hurt you?" Zoey asked.

"It was implied."

Zoey leaped to her feet. Nobody messed with her little brother, no matter how huge he was. It just wasn't right. "Okay, where is this Keith Finch?"

"Over at the quad," Dustin told her, then immediately wished he hadn't. She was probably going to embarrass him. "But Zoey —"

"Come with me," Zoey said, grabbing Dustin's hand

and pulling him away from the table. Dustin didn't even have time to gather his books.

"Zoey!" he protested. "What are you gonna say?"

"Oh, I've got a lot to say," Zoey assured him. She couldn't wait to chew Keith out. What kind of bully made little kids do their homework?

Dustin winced. This was exactly what he was worried about. Things were bad before. Now they were about to get worse.

It took Zoey about two minutes to drag Dustin over to the quad. The area was packed with kids — playing, studying, just hanging out. Zoey scanned the quad for a kid who looked like a jerk. . . .

"Okay, where is he?" she demanded.

"Forget it," Dustin said, half begging. "You'll just make him madder!" He suddenly felt a desperate need to make his sister understand.

Zoey wasn't about to give up that easily. Someone had to teach Keith a lesson! A girl wearing flip-flops and a blue tank walked past.

"'Scuse me — where's Keith Finch?" Zoey asked.

The girl pointed to a kid with a skull-and-crossbones on his black T-shirt. He was hanging out at a table with a couple of guys and a boom box blaring metal music.

Still pulling her little brother by the hand, Zoey marched up to Keith's table and turned off the tunes.

"Hey!" Keith objected. "I was listening to that." He looked a little surprised, like nobody usually messed with his music — especially not a pretty girl in a pink T-shirt.

"You think you can push my little brother around?" Zoey said, ignoring Keith's size and glare. She felt a little like a mama grizzly protecting her cub.

"Zoey, he's very hostile," Dustin warned, looking around. A lot of kids had gathered around.

"Who are you?" Keith asked, eyeing Zoey.

"I'm his sister, and you're gonna leave him alone!" Zoey was not messing around. She stared at Keith, daring him to say something.

Keith stared at Zoey like she had three eyes and a warty nose. Zoey didn't flinch. Everyone in the quad was staring at them, but she didn't care. She had to get Keith off Dustin's back.

"Zoey," a familiar voice whispered behind her. It was Chase, and he tugged on her pink bull's-eye T-shirt. "This may not be the best idea."

"I don't care," Zoey said loudly. What was Chase doing butting in, anyway? She looked around for a way to make her point and spotted something sticking out of a nearby backpack. A tennis racket. Perfect. She grabbed the racket and waved it in front of Keith's face. "You bother him again, you're gonna deal with me," she threatened.

One of the boys sitting next to Keith — the one with short red hair — held up his hands in mock defense. "Ooooh, watch out, dude. The kid's got a bodyguard."

Keith smirked at Zoey. "C'mon," he said, getting to his feet. "We better get outta here before we get served." He laughed at his own joke, leading his cohorts away.

Zoey watched them go, feeling a little bit satisfied. They were retreating, weren't they?

One boy turned back, still laughing. "Hey, Dustin, Mr. Friedman gave me a C on my history quiz. Can you get your sister to beat him up for me?"

Half the kids in the quad laughed, and Dustin felt his cheeks flush. How could his sister do this to him? Now the whole school thought he was a baby! This was his worst nightmare, and Dustin couldn't take any more. He took off.

Zoey caught the look on his face before he bolted. He was definitely not happy. But why? She had protected him from Keith.

Shooting Chase a look, Zoey sighed and went after Dustin.

A few minutes later, Zoey found Dustin sitting by himself at the edge of a staircase.

"There you are," she said, relieved to have found him.

"Leave me alone," Dustin said angrily.

"Dustin!" Zoey said. What was his problem?

"You embarrassed me in front of everyone!" Dustin accused.

"I was *helping* you!" Zoey shot back.

"Well, quit it!"

Zoey sighed. She couldn't do that. "I'm your sister," she started to explain.

"I don't care!" Dustin shouted. "I'm tired of you treating me like a baby! I liked it better at PCA when you weren't here!" He pulled a Bing Bong out of his pocket and waved it in front of Zoey's face. "And I'm eating this Bing Bong!" he screamed, taking a huge bite. He chewed for a second. "Ha!" he finished, his mouth still full. Then he stormed away.

Zoey stared after her brother, her jaw hanging open and her dark eyes full of confusion. She was trying to help, couldn't Dustin see that? Where had she gone wrong?

Elvis Has Left the Building

Zoey flopped down on the grass next to Chase. Behind them, the fountain gurgled. The birds were singing in the trees. Zoey was even wearing her favorite jeans and red tank. Still, she felt lousy.

"Hi." Chase looked up from his book.

"Hi," Zoey sighed.

"You upset about Dustin?" Chase asked.

She was. She was hoping Chase was going to cheer her up, but wasn't sure she wanted to talk about it. "No. I just wanna sit. Go ahead, read your book."

"Okay." Chase shrugged. He turned back to his reading. But before he could even read a whole sentence, Zoey grabbed the book out of his hands.

"How can you read a book when I'm so upset?!" she asked accusingly. Okay, so maybe she really did want to talk about it. Couldn't Chase tell that?

“Sorry. I should be more sensitive,” Chase apologized. He knew an apology went a long way. But he wasn’t quite sure what he was apologizing for. Hadn’t Zoey just told him to go ahead and keep reading?

“Why is Dustin so mad at me? I stood up for him!” Zoey said miserably. Maybe Chase could explain Dustin to her. After all, they were both boys.

“Look,” Chase sighed. “I know it sounds weird, but a kid would rather be hassled by a jerk than have his sister fight his battles for him, ya know?”

Zoey squinted at her friend. “That makes no sense,” she said. Who in their right mind would choose to be hassled by a bully?

“It’s a guy thing.” Chase shrugged again. He wasn’t sure he could explain this to Zoey. And anyway, she didn’t seem like she *wanted* him to explain it to her.

“Then guys are idiots,” Zoey said. She felt kind of bad for insulting the opposite sex, especially since she knew what she was saying wasn’t *totally* true. But she was fed up.

“I’m not denying that.” Chase threw up his hands. What could he say? He didn’t always know why he acted the way he did. But he did know that sometimes he had no choice. “But sometimes you gotta just . . . let a dude be a dude.”

Zoey felt suddenly grateful she was born a girl. "So I can never help him?" she asked.

"No, you can" — Chase wasn't sure how to put it so Zoey wouldn't overdo it — "every once in a while. Just try to keep it on the DL."

Zoey was quiet. Chase leaned over. "Down low," he explained.

"I know what it means." Zoey rolled her eyes. Did he think she'd never heard an acronym before she got to PCA? But right now she had bigger problems to work out. Like how was she going to protect Dustin if she wasn't allowed to get involved? "I just don't ever want to see Dustin get hurt." Zoey sighed.

Chase sighed, too. He didn't like to see Zoey upset. Her heart was in the right place, but he had to keep her from making things worse for Dustin. The poor kid had already been humiliated. "Everyone gets hurt sometimes. You've never been hurt?"

"No, not by a big, dumb bully." Zoey still sounded totally mad.

"Then maybe it's time!" Chase cracked his knuckles, threw an arm around Zoey's neck, got her in a headlock, and pulled her in for the noogie of a lifetime. "Oh, yeah, that's right. She's in trouble now! Gimme your lunch money!"

Zoey couldn't help but laugh. "Quit it," she cried. She grabbed Chase's hand and tried to get out of the hold.

"You gimme your lunch money or I'll — owww!" Chase released Zoey and inspected his pinky. "Did you just *bite* me?"

"Maybe." Zoey looked coy. That's what he got for messing up her twisted ponytail.

The look of fake shock on Chase's face was worth it. He stared at Zoey with mock dismay and wagged a finger at her. "Ohhhh, it's on!" he said, jumping to his feet.

Zoey was not about to suffer another noogie. She leaped up and ran all the way to the girls' lounge. Chase hadn't solved her problems, but he had made her laugh. Zoey pushed open the door and casually walked into the lounge. Chase stumbled in right behind her, out of breath.

"Whoa, you're fast," he panted.

"Maybe you're just slow," Zoey shot back.

"Harsh." Chase hoped that Dana and Michael hadn't caught that dig. Luckily they weren't paying any attention. They were just sitting on one of the couches, talking.

Suddenly a pink blur holding a hair dryer came flying down the stairs — Nicole. "Guys! Guys . . ." The girl was clearly in a panic. "Our dorm advisor took Elvis."

"She took our dog?" Chase had only just caught his breath and now he felt like the wind had been knocked out of him. Dana and Michael hurried over to hear.

"How'd she find him?" Michael asked.

"Well, I went to the bathroom to check my hair"—Nicole ran her fingers through her long dark hair to demonstrate—"because sometimes it frizzes and I hate it when it frizzes—"

Zoey grabbed her roomie with both hands — now was not the time for a full debriefing on the hazards of frizz. The D.A. had taken Elvis! "What happened?!" she demanded.

"When I opened the door Elvis ran out, and before I could do anything the D.A. grabbed him. . . ." Nicole looked like she couldn't go on. There was something else she was afraid to say. Dana, Zoey, Chase, and Michael waited for her to spit it out.

"*And . . .*" Michael prompted.

Nicole winced. She really didn't want to tell them the last part . . . it was too terrible! But she had no choice. "She's taking him to the animal shelter!"

Zoey felt like someone had just knocked her down. First her trouble with Dustin, and now this!

Plan B

Dustin was busy playing a video game. The hand-held game he was playing beeped and his score tripled. Awesome. This was the most fun he'd had in days. He'd decided not to work on homework — not anyone's homework . . . just for a little while. He'd even taken a shower and put on clean clothes — an orange-and-blue rugby shirt and jeans. Now he was kicking back, taking a load off.

Unfortunately, Dustin's moment of freedom was about to end. Keith Finch and his two sidekick thugs walked slowly toward him. Keith was wearing a T-shirt with a venomous snake on it that looked like it was about to strike.

"What's up, Dustin?" Keith's voice was all cute and friendly.

Dustin didn't buy it — Keith was anything but cute

and friendly. Dustin sighed. Well, he *had* been having fun. "Look, Keith. Just leave me alone."

"And what if I don't? Your sister's gonna beat me up?"

His buddies cracked up. Dustin had no reply. What could he say? The terrible truth was that Zoey had actually threatened Keith. Unbelievable.

"Listen, punk . . ." Keith leaned in. Dustin leaned back for some air. "From now on you're doin' my homework *and* my laundry." Keith launched a huge bag filled with dirty clothes. It landed on the table in front of Dustin.

Dustin could not believe his ears. He stood up. "C'mon, Keith . . ." He could not be serious!

"Uh-oh! He's on his feet." Keith's redheaded friend shook with mock fear.

"Watch out," Keith's other friend joked. "He might whip out his cell phone and call his sister for backup!"

"Oooh," Keith squealed like he was frightened before putting his hands out for high fives from his friends. The three walked away, cracking up. They left Keith's big bag of laundry behind.

"Look at that!" Michael leaned on the arm of the couch in his dorm room, checking out the image on the screen of Chase's laptop. He could not believe what he saw.

"Do you see that?" Chase asked, pointing at the screen.

"That's insane."

"That's impossible."

"That's . . ."

Suddenly the door to their room opened and Dustin walked in, slamming it behind him. "I need some advice," he announced.

"On what?" Michael had noticed that the little dude was looking pretty somber lately, not to mention totally wiped out.

"On how to handle a jerk!" Dustin said.

Michael and Chase looked at each other, nodded, and looked back at Dustin. They were both smiling.

"We can help you with that," Chase said.

"Yes we can," Michael agreed.

"You told him *what*?!" Zoey could not believe her ears. She thought Chase was her friend. She thought he was helping her out. She thought he cared about protecting her little brother as much as she did.

Chase winced. This was not going too great so far. "Well, ya know," Chase tried to explain, "sometimes you gotta stand up to a guy like Keith." He made a fist and pumped it in the air. "Tell him off."

Zoey stared at him. Did he realize he was talking about her four-and-a-half-foot-tall brother and an eighth grader the size of a moose? There was someone Zoey would like to tell off, and he was sitting right next to her on the couch in the lounge. She punched Chase on the shoulder instead.

"Okay," Chase started, "what has this shoulder done to you?" It was the same shoulder she had gone after the other day and it was still sore from the first incident.

Zoey had backed off of Dustin a little, and now where were they? Her brother was probably about to get pummeled by a giant jerk, that's where. And that was not cool.

If nobody was going to help her, Zoey was going to have to take care of Dustin herself. Right now. She got to her feet and headed for the door.

"Where are you going?"

"To help Dustin," Zoey replied. Hadn't he been paying attention?

"No, no, no, no, no . . ." Chase had to stop her. Zoey was a smart girl, but obviously clueless about how much damage she could do to the little guy's reputation. "You cannot do that."

"I'm not letting my baby brother stand up to a dumb jerk who's twice his size!" Zoey shot back hotly.

"Listen," Chase said as calmly as he could. There had to be a way to make her understand. "Whatever Keith does to him — it's better than having every kid in the school laughing at him 'cause his big sister has to be his bodyguard."

Taking a deep breath, Zoey let that sink in for a sec. As stupid as risking getting beat up seemed, she had to admit that Chase had a point. *It's a guy thing,* Zoey told herself. But maybe there was something a girl could still do to help. "Fine," she said to Chase. "Come with me."

Chase looked baffled. "Where?"

"I have ideas." Zoey raised her eyebrows.

"Zoey." Chase knew all about Zoey's ideas. . . .

"Now." Zoey grabbed Chase by the neck of his black-and-white polo shirt and pulled him out of the lounge.

"I finished grading your homework assignments." Mr. Kirby strolled between the desks in geometry class, handing back homework. He was cool, calm, and collected as always. Dustin admired that about his math teacher. Rumor had it he surfed every morning before school — maybe that was what made him so Zen. As for Dustin, he was feeling anything but Zen. He was tired from staying up doing homework and laundry. He was jittery from too much coffee. And he had a bad feeling in the pit of his stomach, either from being tortured, humiliated, or his regular diet of Bing Bongs.

"Keith, you did some very good work. Much improved." Mr. Kirby handed Keith his paper. Dustin resisted the urge to pat himself on the back. Even sleep deprived, he was smarter than that jerk. Now if only he was big enough to wipe the evil smile off Keith's face.

"'Scuse me, Mr. Kirby?"

Dustin was so busy thinking of all the things he wanted to do to Keith that he didn't hear Michael come in. He handed Mr. Kirby a note and left quickly.

The teacher glanced at the slip of paper. "Keith, it seems you're wanted in the principal's office," he said smoothly.

A chorus of "oooohs" filled the math room as Keith stood to go. Keith was busted!

"Ah! No need to 'oooh.'" Mr. Kirby shook his head as Keith headed for the door.

On the way out, Keith gave Dustin a dirty look. Dustin was as happy as anyone to see the thug get busted. But what was he getting busted for?

* * *

Keith cautiously opened the door to the principal's office. He'd been here before, but usually he knew what he was sent for. Today, it was a mystery. Sure, he'd been getting a little help with his homework . . . and his laundry. But nobody knew anything about that except for that shrimp Dustin, and his friends, who would never rat him out. A man he had never seen before was sitting behind the principal's desk. He had a mustache, glasses, and a very angry look in his eyes.

"Close the door and sit down," the man ordered.

He obviously meant business. Keith closed the door and sat.

"I'm very upset with you, Mr. Finch," the man said sternly, sounding a lot like Keith's dad. But Keith had never seen this guy before. Who was he?

"You're not the principal," Keith said slowly, hoping the man would identify himself. Was he some kind of cop?

"No back sass!" the man bellowed.

"Who are you?" Keith asked.

"I happen to be the Dean of Discipline," the man growled. He pushed himself up from his desk and circled slowly to the other side, buttoning his suit.

There was a Dean of Discipline at PCA? Keith

opened his mouth to ask what exactly that was. But before he could get three words out, the dean was all over him.

"Stop speaking!" he demanded loudly.

"Okay." Keith wanted to ask why he was here but thought better of it. He seemed to be in hot water. The less he said, the better.

The dean paced in the small office like a caged and hungry tiger. "I understand you've been harassing some of the younger students. Is that correct?" He paused in front of Keith's chair and stared into his eyes.

"W-well —" Keith stammered nervously. He racked his brain to think of a way out of this one.

"Don't even think about lying," the dean growled.

There was no fooling this guy. And Keith couldn't think of a good enough lie, anyway. "Yeah, I guess I have."

"You guess?" the dean echoed, his voice dripping with angry sarcasm.

"Yes," Keith admitted.

"Yes what?! C'mon, say it, Finch! Tell me!" The dean loomed over Finch's chair. He was so close, Keith couldn't think straight.

"I . . . I . . . I pick on people!" Keith blurted nervously. The office went quiet. Keith waited for the ax to fall.

"You mean, you *used* to." The dean's voice was low and intimidating.

"Huh?" Keith was bewildered.

The dean bent down. He put his face so close to Keith's that he could feel his hot breath. The dean pointed a finger right in his face. "If I ever hear of you bothering any student on the PCA campus — especially younger ones — I'll expel you faster than pigtails on a giraffe, do you understand me?" Flecks of spit flew out of the dean's mouth and hit Keith in the face.

"Yes, sir." Keith got the message loud and moist and clear. "Except for the giraffe part."

"Get out!" the dean bellowed, straightening.

"Yes, sir!" Keith was only too happy to go. He bailed out of his chair, made for the door, and slammed it behind him.

From their hiding spot under the window outside, Zoey and Chase had heard everything. They rushed in through the other door the minute they heard Keith leave.

"Herb, you were great!" Zoey congratulated the janitor. She knew he could do Shakespeare, but she didn't know he'd be this awesome as the "Dean of Discipline"!

"Yeah! I was outside and you still had me shakin'!" Chase shook his head with disbelief.

Quickly ditching the fake mustache and glasses, Herb transformed from scary dean to friendly janitor in an instant. "Really? I was good?" He hadn't had a role that great in a long time — it was nice to hone his acting skills right on campus.

"That was the best acting any janitor has ever done!" Chase said, totally blown away. And he had to admit, this was one of Zoey's best ideas yet!

"Thanks!" Herb grinned. Zoey and Chase grinned back. "Now, if you'll excuse me, there's a clogged toilet in the gym calling my name."

Eww. Herb made a hasty exit with a plunger as Chase's and Zoey's smiles faded.

You Tell Him

The lousy feeling in Dustin's stomach was getting worse. He couldn't even have fun hanging with his friends — he was too preoccupied with his problems with Keith. Chase and Michael were right. A dude had to do what a dude had to do. And Dustin definitely had something to do.

"Hey . . . here he comes." Dustin's friend gave him a warning. But Dustin had already seen what was coming — Keith. Dustin took a deep breath as the bully lumbered down the steps toward him.

"Are you sure you want to do this?" his friend asked, his dark eyes wide.

No, Dustin thought. But he was as ready as he was ever going to be. "Yeah," he answered, taking a long drink of his soda for strength.

Dustin took a few steps toward his enemy. He was so focused on Keith that he didn't notice the crowd growing in the quad. He didn't even see Chase and Zoey coming around the corner or ducking back behind the PCA sign to watch.

"Hey, Dustin —" Keith began to say.

Dustin cut him off. "Just be quiet!" he said in his toughest voice. Inside he was quaking, but he was not going to be bullied by Keith anymore. It was time to tell him off.

"Huh?" Keith was baffled. "Look, I just came here to tell you —"

"I'm sick of you, Keith Finch," Dustin said, cutting him off a second time. "I'm sick of you pushin' me around!"

"Dude —" Keith tried to get a word in.

"From now on, you do your own homework."

"Look, man —"

"And I'm not doing your stupid laundry, 'cause it smells bad — like you." Dustin could barely believe his own mouth. The other kids in the quad looked pretty shocked, too.

Behind the wall, Zoey turned to Chase. Her ideas might be good, but apparently his advice had not been so bad, either. She'd never seen her little brother like this before! Of course, the "Dean of Discipline" had already put the fear in Finch. But Dustin was something else!

"From now on, just leave me alone. Got it?" Dustin finished.

"Yeah. Sure. Okay," Keith said, raising his hands and backing away.

It was totally unbelievable. Dustin watched Keith's back as he walked away. He had done it. He'd actually told off Keith Finch! His friends and a few other kids who had seen the whole thing gathered around Dustin. They patted him on the back and congratulated him.

"Whoa, that was awesome. He totally backed down!"

"C'mon, let's go celebrate!" one of Dustin's friends suggested.

Dustin shook his head. He was in shock. A Bing Bong and soda would taste good, but right now, Dustin had something more . . . uh, urgent to take care of.

"Nah." He waved the other kids off. "I think I'm just gonna go change my underwear."

Zoey looked around her dorm room and smiled. Things were finally looking up — way up. Sitting on the arm of the couch, she listened as Chase filled Nicole and

Michael in on everything that had happened that afternoon, especially Dustin's showdown with Keith.

Chase grinned. "And then he goes, 'And your stupid laundry smells bad — like you,'" he said, hamming it up a little. This was one of the best stories he'd told in a long time. Plus, it was true!

"No way!" Michael was loving it. Dustin had taken their advice and run with it!

Zoey took a swig of soda. She had played and replayed the scene in her head all afternoon, and was still psyched to hear Chase tell it to their friends. Dustin really made that bully back down, and with only a little help from her.

"Seriously?" As she stood up and grabbed some soda out of the mini fridge, Nicole tried to imagine Dustin and Keith facing off.

"Yeah! It was so awesome." Zoey hadn't felt this proud since Dustin got into geometry class early.

Suddenly the door opened, and Dana walked in carrying a blue fleece blanket. Zoey thought she looked great in a black-and-purple top and black jeans, but what was with the heavy blanket?

"What's up, guys?" Dana asked. She casually lifted back the blanket to reveal a familiar brown nose, a white fuzzy face, and two brown ears.

"Elvis!" everyone cheered, jumping up off the couch. Chase couldn't believe it. He'd been worried that Elvis might be gone for good.

Michael scooped him up, blanket and all, and gave him a good scratch. "Hey, guy." Michael's face lit up. He had really missed his little room-mutt.

"How'd you get him back?" Chase was so happy to see Elvis, *his* tail was practically wagging.

Dana shrugged, totally aloof. "I snuck off campus, took a bus to the animal shelter, and got him back." She said it like it was no big deal.

Zoey stared, dumbfounded. Sneaking off campus? For a dog? Dana? Well, maybe the sneaking off part . . .

"Aw, see?" Zoey cooed. "You *do* love him!" This was proof positive of Dana's mushy side.

"I think she does," Chase agreed.

"I do not," Dana scowled. She tried to look insulted.

"Yes, you do." Nicole started to chant, "Dana loves Elvis! Dana loves Elvis!" Zoey joined in. There was no denying it. Michael held Elvis close and swayed with him back and forth. The little dog was irresistible.

"Okay!" Dana relented. She did like the little guy — a lot, actually. "But if any of you"— Dana pointed around the room —"tells anyone I did something nice, I will mess you up!" After all, she had a reputation to uphold.

Michael, Chase, and Zoey smiled as Dana stomped out, slamming the door behind her. Her secret was safe.

Everyone crowded around Elvis, petting him and scratching his ears.

A second later, Dana stuck her head back into the room. "D.A.'s coming!" she warned.

"What do we do?" Michael panicked. They could not lose Elvis again!

Zoey and Nicole looked at each other. There was only one way to get out of this one.

"The trick!" Nicole held up her finger.

"What trick?" Chase was baffled.

"We taught him a trick!" Zoey said quickly. There was no time to explain.

"Put him down!" Nicole said to Michael, glancing from Elvis to the door and back.

Zoey waited until Elvis had four on the floor. "Ready, Elvis? Hide!" She hoped it would work. Elvis looked at Zoey for a second, then walked over to a pile of stuffed animals, lay down, and held perfectly still. He obviously remembered the trick, and surrounded by toys, he looked exactly like a little plush puppy. And just in time.

Coco, their dorm advisor, walked right in without knocking and gazed around the room. She looked annoyed.

"Hi, Coco," they all greeted her. Zoey tried to look casual. They couldn't lose Elvis again!

Coco just kept looking around the room, like she wanted to find something to bust them on.

Finally Coco said something. "So . . . looks like we have a problem here, don't we?" She raised her eyebrows.

Zoey couldn't believe she'd spotted Elvis. He was staying so still — just like they taught him.

"Problem?" Nicole echoed, giving Coco an innocent smile. Sometimes having a reputation for being a space case came in handy.

"You know the PCA rule," Coco said, as if she were talking to little kids. Chase and Michael looked totally nervous. The game was up.

"No boys in the girls' dorm after eight, okay?" Coco looked at her watch impatiently. ". . . And it's eight-oh-four."

Zoey had never seen two guys more relieved to be busted. Michael and Chase held up their hands like caught criminals.

"We're on our way out," Chase said.

"Yeah, we'll soon be a memory," Michael added.

Coco gave them all one last annoyed look over her shoulder. "Hurry," she said before the door closed.

As soon as the door clicked shut, everyone took a deep breath. That was close!

"C'mere, Elvis!" Zoey held out her arms and Elvis jumped into them. He had done as good an acting job as Herb the janitor! "Good boy! Yes, you are. . . ."

"Who did good? You did!" Nicole crooned, scratching his floppy ears.

"This is really good bottled water," Nicole said, looking over the label. It was yet another gorgeous day at PCA, and Zoey, Nicole, and Chase were on their way to class.

Zoey shot Nicole a sideways glance. Was she for real? Nicole could go off on the weirdest stuff. "It's just water," she reminded her.

"I hate water." Chase pedaled his bike slowly next to the girls. He tried to avoid water whenever he could — too bland. He was a soda man.

Zoey rolled her eyes behind her red-tinted sunglasses. They matched her red varsity T-shirt and her retro red-and-white-checked belt.

Zoey waited for Nicole's next H_2O insight, but

instead Nicole motioned with her eyes to someone coming down the path. It was Dustin.

“Hello, Zoey,” Dustin spoke formally, like they were acquaintances who hadn’t seen each other in a long time. In fact, he hadn’t seen his sister since he told Keith to take a hike. A lot had gone on and, well, Dustin had to admit that he really missed her.

“Hi,” Zoey replied, taking off her sunglasses. She wasn’t sure what to say next, so she just got right to the point. “You still hate me?”

Dustin let her squirm for a second. She had really, really embarrassed him. “Nah. You were just tryin’ to help out,” he finally said with a shrug.

Zoey grinned. “Thanks. And I promise I’ll let you fight your own battles from now on.”

“Okay. But . . .” Dustin didn’t want Zoey to leave him *totally* alone. “Would you still try and make me look cooler?”

Nicole laughed, relieved that Dustin and Zoey were back on track, and that Dustin had the sense to take Zoey up on her fashion advice. She had consulted Zoey just that morning, and had ended up in an awesome pink T-shirt with green piping on the sleeves and an equally awesome green skirt with a matching belt.

Zoey looked at her brother. He really did need her help. He looked way too . . . neat.

"I'll take his shirt," Zoey said to Nicole. "You take his hair." Zoey untucked Dustin's dark blue, long-sleeve button-down while Nicole quickly mussed his shaggy blond hair.

"Socks," Chase reminded them.

"Oh, yeah." Zoey quickly scrunched them down toward his sneakers. "There. All cool."

"Thanks." Dustin smiled. He felt better already. Over Zoey's shoulder he spotted some of his friends. "Later." He waved. "Hey, guys, wait up!"

Zoey watched her little brother race away. One of his shoelaces was flopping around. He could trip! "Wait," Zoey called after him. "Tie your shoelace! Dustin! Dus —"

Nicole reached out and put her hand over Zoey's mouth. Would she ever learn?

Zoey bit her tongue.

"Just keep walkin'," Chase said. Nicole and Chase pushed Zoey down the path. Maybe they were right. Maybe she did baby Dustin. But he *was* her baby brother. Zoey smiled to herself as she saw Herb sweeping the path and practicing his Shakespeare. If he could act like a dean, maybe she could act more like a sister and not so much like a mom.

More Drama

In the arts building, Zoey sat next to Nicole in the front row of the drama classroom. Only it wasn't really a classroom — it was more like a small theater. Rows of chairs took up one half, while a stage covered with pillows, furniture, and props took up the other. Mr. Fletcher, the drama teacher, stood in front of the stage. With thinning reddish-blond hair, reading glasses, and a gray vest, he looked sort of . . . conservative. But Mr. Fletcher had an artsy side that showed itself regularly.

Since Keith had stopped harassing her little brother, things were getting back to normal at PCA, which was a relief. Zoey was loving her new school, but there was a lot to keep up with: friends, schoolwork, basketball practice, taking care of Elvis . . . the list was long. And now there was something else to add: the school play!

"Okay, before you all go, I'd like to talk to you about our annual fall production," Mr. Fletcher said, peering at the class over the tops of his half-glasses. Zoey grinned. Mr. Fletcher could not hide his excitement. He was so thrilled about the play, he looked like a kid with an ice-cream cone.

"Please say *Annie*, please say *Annie*, please say *Annie*. . . ." Behind her, a kid named Mark started mumbling to himself. He had his thick fingers crossed and was waving them in the air. Zoey gave Chase — who was sitting next to Mark — a look. Mark didn't seem like the kind of guy who would want to put on a musical about an orphaned redhead, but was obviously some kind of *Annie* freak.

Mr. Fletcher waved his hands around dramatically. "I am so excited to announce that this year we are going to be doing a play written as a homework assignment by one of our very own students — Mr. Chase Matthews!" He beamed and extended one of his arms toward Chase with flare.

A bunch of kids in the class clapped and whooped it up.

"Yeah, Chase!" a kid cheered.

"Woo-woo!" someone else shouted.

Chase nodded and waved his hands dismissively,

feeling kind of embarrassed. He'd written the play and really liked it. But what if everyone else — like Zoey, for instance — thought it was lame?

Zoey turned around to smile at Chase, who looked like his usual self in a dark red T-shirt, baggy button-down, and cargo shorts. He hadn't said anything about writing a play. How cool!

The only one not cheering was Mark, the *Annie* freak. He glared at Chase like he was dirt. Luckily, the bell rang. Chase was off the hook, at least for the moment.

"Bell . . ." Mr. Fletcher mumbled. "Remember, auditions start today at three," he reminded everyone as they filed out of the classroom.

Mark stopped right in front of Chase. His blue-striped polo shirt was untucked, and he looked kind of . . . scary. "I wanted to be Annie," he growled, hoisting his yellow backpack on his back and brushing by.

Chase gave Nicole and Zoey a look.

Chase, Nicole, and Zoey headed out into the California sun. Chase had been going to PCA for a couple of years but was still blown away by what an awesome place it was. The ocean alone was enough to make up for the schoolwork — almost.

"So, what's your play about?" Zoey asked as they walked down the path. She had to admit it: Since she started drama class she'd been bitten by the acting bug. She was definitely going to audition for the play and was dying to know all about it.

"Well . . ." Chase hesitated. He had to make it sound good. "It's kind of a classic love story. See, this spaceship crashes to Earth, and this female alien gets rescued by a lifeguard." He stole a look at Zoey to see if she liked the idea. She looked great today in a light blue silk-screened T-shirt, a blue-flowered skirt, and sneakers.

Nicole's eyes were wide with admiration. Writing a play had to take a lot of work — and creativity. "And you're playing the lifeguard?" she asked, raising an eyebrow.

Chase nodded. "Yes, I am."

"Well, I'm trying out for the role of the female alien," Zoey said, feeling a twinge of excitement. Her brown eyes were bright. Maybe it was because Chase had written the play. Or maybe she'd been inspired by janitor Herb's role as the "Dean of Discipline." Whatever the reason, she couldn't wait until auditions that afternoon.

"Me, too!" Nicole said, her straight dark hair blowing a little in the breeze. Playing an alien sounded like fun.

"Cool," Chase said. Finally, real girls to play the

girls' parts! "'Cause, ya know, this is the first year at PCA that we've ever had girls to audition."

Nicole tilted her head to one side. She hadn't thought of that. "Oh, yeah," she said.

Zoey stopped for a second. "Who used to play the female roles before PCA let girls in?" she asked.

Chase stared at Zoey. Did she have to ask that? Images flashed in his head — and one in particular. There he was onstage, dressed in a yellow-and-white cheerleader outfit, complete with a pleated miniskirt and an itchy blond ponytail wig that looked questionable at best.

"Yay, oh, yay!" Chase heard himself cheer. Ugh. He'd heard about that one from the guys for the rest of the year. They'd called him Cheerleader Chase, yelling it to him all over campus. It was a total nightmare. Luckily everyone seemed to forget about it over the summer. And he would never have to play a female role again.

Chase cleared his throat. "I'd rather not talk about it," he admitted.

Zoey and Nicole tried not to laugh too hard. Zoey had a pretty good idea what the answer to her question was, but decided not to hassle her friend on this one.

"Well, I think it's awesome that you wrote a play,"

Zoey said, smiling. Chase was such a cool guy — he did so many different things and wasn't afraid to be himself.

"Yeah," Nicole agreed. "I can't believe you didn't tell us."

"Ah," Chase said with a nod. It was true. He hadn't breathed a word about the play to anyone. "I guess I was worried that people might not think it's cool," he admitted. Zoey and Nicole were one thing. Some of his guy friends at PCA were something else.

Nicole gave Chase an "are you kidding?" look. Who wouldn't think that writing an entire play wasn't cool? "Puh-lease," she said.

Zoey nodded emphatically and held up a hand. "Totally cool," she echoed.

"That is so uncool!" Logan said with a knowing smirk as he pulled on a black sneaker. He couldn't believe he lived with a guy who would spend hours and hours writing a dumb play for a homework assignment — and then actually want to be in it!

Chase looked up from his silver laptop with a grimace. "Thank you," he said sarcastically. "That's very nice."

Michael slid onto the couch next to Chase. "I think it's cool," he said. "I'm gonna try out."

"You should," Chase agreed, grateful for his other roomie's input. Michael was never afraid to offer his opinion, even when he disagreed with Logan.

"Awww, how cute," Logan mocked. "Chase and Michael are going to be in a little play together. When do we go skirt shopping?" He laughed at his own joke.

Chase scowled at Logan. He could be such a jerk. "Okay, make fun of it all you want, dude. Everyone else thinks it's cool."

Logan shook his head and bent down to tie his other shoe. "Why do you waste your time with the drama club? Why don't you go out for football or somethin'?"

Because I'm lousy at football, Chase thought. But he couldn't admit that to Logan. Logan was good at every kind of sport there was. It was actually a little annoying.

"'Cause the drama club's loaded with girls," Chase replied, glad to have an answer that was not only true but that Logan would be down with. "And I've seen the football team." Chase raised an eyebrow.

Next, Please!

Dustin let out a hacking cough and plodded to Zoey's dorm room door. He felt too miserable to bother changing out of his navy blue jammies and slippers. His nose was stuffy, his head throbbed, and he coughed every two seconds.

Dustin raised a feeble hand and knocked on Zoey's door. A second later Dana opened it.

"Hey," Dustin said, feeling exhausted. Being sick was the pits. He was hoping Zoey would give him some advice or medicine . . . or something healthy to eat. "Hey, is Zoey here?"

"Nope," Dana replied. She was listening to her favorite band and was a little annoyed by the interruption. With two roommates, she didn't get much time to herself, so she loved to take advantage of every minute she got.

Dustin's shoulders sagged. "Do you know where she is?" he asked.

"Nope," Dana repeated. She didn't have time for this! She wasn't Zoey's keeper.

"'Cause I'm sick, and I was wondering —"

Dana didn't wait to hear the rest of Dustin's sob story. Just last week the kid was complaining that Zoey acted like she was his mother. And now he was coming to her because he was sick? Feeling only a tiny bit guilty, she closed the door before he finished talking.

Dustin stared at the dry-erase board on the door in front of him. Where was his sister when he needed her? Oh, well. He'd have to make do with his last few gummy worms. He turned to head back to his dorm and saw Quinn — that weird girl who was always doing experiments — standing in front of him. Zoey had roomed with Quinn for a few days the second week of school when she was having roommate trouble, and had some interesting stories to tell. Quinn was looking at him kind of funny, like she had an idea. . . .

"Hi, Dustin," she said with an odd smile. Her six long, skinny braids bobbed a little.

"Hey, Quinn."

"Did you just say you were sick?" she asked,

peering at him. If Dustin was sick, she could try out her latest experiments on him — on a real, live person!

Dustin suddenly had an uneasy feeling . . . like he should run. The problem was, he was too tired. "Yeah, I got a cold and I can't find Zoey," he explained.

Quinn grabbed ahold of Dustin's shoulders and leaned in close to examine his face. She could do a lot more for him than his sister, Zoey. She could cure him! "Do you have fever? Phlegm? Mucus? Germs?" she rattled off.

Dustin shrugged. "I guess," he said. This was starting to get creepy.

"Excellent," Quinn said, straightening up. Dustin was an absolutely perfect specimen.

"Huh?" Dustin said. His head felt kind of . . . foggy. Did Quinn just say his symptoms were excellent?

Quinn nodded. "I can cure you," she said excitedly. "Come with me." She took Dustin by the hand and led him down the hall.

Dustin had no idea what he was in for. But he was too tired and achy to resist. Besides, Quinn was weird but harmless. What could happen?

Zoey sat with a bunch of other girls in the drama classroom waiting to audition. She'd read the script earlier that afternoon and couldn't wait for her turn to try out.

Chase and Mr. Fletcher stood together in front of the stage, welcoming the girls to the audition.

"Afternoon, ladies," Chase greeted. "Thanks for coming down to audition for the play." He smiled, trying to make them all feel welcome. He wanted each of the girls to give her best performance. Secretly he was hoping that Zoey would get the alien part, but he had to be fair. Everyone deserved a chance.

"Let's see," Mr. Fletcher said, peering through his glasses to read the list on his clipboard. "Auditioning first will be Jodi Lockwood."

Jodi smiled and leaped out of her chair excitedly. Her short pigtails bobbed as she hurried up to the stage to take her place beside Chase.

"Oh, and remember," Chase explained. "This play takes place on a beach in Hawaii, and you've just been rescued from the ocean by me, the hot lifeguard." He smiled sheepishly. He didn't really think of himself as hot. But the lifeguard was definitely supposed to be a hottie, and Mr. Fletcher had told him that he should play the lead since it was his play. So for the moment, at least, he got to be hot.

"Um, okay, here we go. Scene G," Chase said. He

glanced down at the script and cleared his throat. He'd never read in front of a bunch of girls, and he wanted to look like he knew what he was doing.

"Wow, you almost drowned," Chase read, trying to sound natural. It wasn't that hard, since he'd written the play. He knew every single line by heart. "Are you okay?"

Jodi held her script by her waist. "I think so!" she yelled. "What planet is this?" Her head bobbed back and forth like a bird searching for worms.

Chase blinked. Why was she screaming? He didn't say the lifeguard was deaf, did he? "You don't know what planet this is?" he asked in a regular voice, shooting her a sideways look.

"No!" Jodi shrieked. "I lost control of my starship and it plunged into the ocean!"

A bunch of the girls in the audience stuck their fingers in their ears to drown out the loud, screechy sound. At the table, Mr. Fletcher shook his head miserably.

Chase couldn't take it anymore. "Uh, why are you screaming?" he asked.

Jodi smiled broadly. "I'm projecting," she explained cheerfully.

Mr. Fletcher looked a little disturbed. "Next," he called.

Marta stood center stage next to Chase, holding

her script close to her blue-and-white-striped sleeveless blouse. Chase hoped Marta wouldn't be a screamer. But he wasn't expecting what came next.

"I lost control of my starship and it plunged into the ocean, so then I started swimming." She sang the whole line like an opera star.

Chase's face pinched together. The girls in the audience shook their heads. At the back of the room, Mr. Fletcher tilted his head to the side. What was she doing?

Marta paused and dropped her script to her side. "This is a musical, right?" she asked, suddenly looking a little embarrassed.

"Not really, no," Chase said.

Marta looked completely disappointed as she turned and walked offstage.

Chase was waiting for Mr. Fletcher to read the name of the next auditionee when Mark strode onto the stage. A few of the girls in the audience laughed out loud, and Chase stared in disbelief. He was wearing a red-and-white dress and a curly red wig. He looked unmistakably like Annie. Weird Annie, but Annie just the same.

Chase wasn't sure if Mark was trying to get back at him for being the reason they were not doing *Annie*, or if Mark's desperation to be Annie had gotten the best of him.

"We're not doing *Annie*," he said flatly.

Silently fuming, Mark turned and walked off the stage.

Chase closed his eyes for a second, trying to banish Annie-Mark from his brain. His eyes flew open when he heard Mr. Fletcher call the next name.

"Zoey Brooks," Mr. Fletcher read from his clipboard.

Zoey felt a little thrill of excitement. She was up! Trying to ignore her nerves, she took the stage next to Chase. Thank goodness the person she got to read with was a good friend.

"You don't know what planet this is?" Chase read, giving Zoey an encouraging look. He really wanted her to do well . . . not that the competition so far was that intense.

"No. I lost control of my starship and it plunged into the ocean. So then I started swimming. . . ." Zoey tried to speak clearly but not raise her voice. They'd all had enough screaming for one day. In the back, Mr. Fletcher leaned forward slightly, watching the actors on the stage.

"Wait, you're an alien?" Chase read.

Zoey nodded. "I am." She barely had to look at her script — the lines came really easily to her. "Thank you for pulling me out of the water."

"Hey, it's my job," Chase said casually. "Besides, it's not every day that an incredibly cute alien girl washes up on my beach."

Zoey smiled shyly. "You think I'm incredibly cute?" she asked.

"I incredibly do," Chase said, smiling back. That was true. He happened to think Zoey was the cutest girl on campus, hands down. And right now she looked especially adorable with her blond hair down and her dazzling smile. And she was a pretty good actress, too.

Mr. Fletcher leaped to his feet, clapping. "Excellent! Bra and vo!"

The kids in the audience seemed to agree.

Chase flashed Zoey a smile. She'd done great, and he was psyched. She'd get the lead for sure! "You were awesome," he told her.

"Thanks," Zoey said. "You were, too."

"Zoey, um, I'll talk it over with Chase and we'll let you know," Mr. Fletcher said.

"Cool," Zoey said with a nod. She'd done her best and would have to wait and see if it was enough. But she had a feeling her chances were good, especially since Nicole had decided to audition for a different part — the hula girl. When she found out she'd get to wear a real grass skirt, she practically screamed.

* * *

Chase leaned back in his chair. He and Mr. Fletcher were reviewing the candidates in the drama club classroom. Chase was pretty sure he knew who he wanted to play each female role, but they needed to make it official.

Mr. Fletcher had a stack of 8-by-10 head shots he'd taken at auditions. He held them up one by one.

"Screamer?" he asked, displaying Jodi's photo.

Chase shook his head. His ears were still ringing. "No way," he said, shaking his unruly curls.

"Annie?" He held up Mark's Annie photo.

"Gross," Chase said, holding up his hands and looking away. Red was really not Mark's color.

Mr. Fletcher wrinkled his nose and nodded. "Agreed, disturbing," he said, clucking his tongue and shuddering slightly. He set down the photo and reached for another, smiling as he held it up.

"Zoey," he said.

"Absolutely," Chase said, trying not to sound too biased. "Clearly the best."

"Agreed." Mr. Fletcher had his mind made up already, too. "So then . . ." He jotted a few notes on a pad of paper. "We'll give the hula girl to Nicole and make Zoey our lead."

Chase felt good all over. Zoey got the part! They both got to play the leads. That meant lots of rehearsing together, practicing lines . . .

"Cool," he said. "Zoey it is. That's . . . that's great," he murmured.

Mr. Fletcher gave Chase a knowing look over the tops of his glasses. Chase felt like he was under the microscope. "Is that because your character shares most of his scenes with Zoey's character?"

Chase's face went blank. Did *everyone* know how he felt about Zoey? "Of course not," he fibbed.

Mr. Fletcher gave Chase a "yeah, right" look. "Mmm-hmmm," he said doubtfully.

"Seriously," Chase said as convincingly as he could.

"Whatever," Mr. Fletcher said, shrugging and getting to his feet. "I'm going to go bring in the boys to audition." He disappeared out the classroom door.

Chase looked down at Zoey's picture. Her dazzling smile was all for him, the hot lifeguard. "Zoey's playing the cute alien!" he sang, grinning from ear to ear.

Sucked Under Quicksand

Across campus, Dustin looked warily around Quinn's room. Zoey wasn't kidding — it was *full* of weird stuff. Colored concoctions bubbled all over the place. Electronic devices beeped and flashed. Contraptions of every shape and size were strewn on the floor and the bed. Dustin could not believe Zoey had actually *lived* here.

Quinn sat Dustin down on the bed. "Okay, Dustin," she said in her squeaky voice. "Tell me exactly what's wrong with you." She peered at him through her glasses.

"Well, I have a cough." He coughed a couple of times to demonstrate. "And a runny nose and I think I have a fever," he said. That about summed it up.

"Perfect," Quinn said. Several of her long braids seemed to quiver with excitement. She finally had a real, live specimen right here in her own room! She hadn't had one of those since Zoey moved out the second week of school, and Zoey had been very reluctant. "I'll have you cured in no time."

Dustin watched Quinn pull out a large contraption that looked like a vacuum cleaner with a smaller hose at the end. "Stick out your tongue," she instructed.

Dustin wasn't sure about this but was a tiny bit curious as to whether Quinn could actually cure him.

He stuck out his tongue. "Ahhhhh . . ."

Quinn switched on her contraption, raised the hose to Dustin's mouth, and stuck it right on his tongue.

"*Gauughh!*" Dustin gurgled. "What are you doing?" he said as well as he could with a sucking hose on his tongue.

"Oh, this is a tongue vacuum," Quinn said loudly over the machine. It was one of her more recent Quinnventions. She was quite proud of it. And in a minute she'd know if it worked!

Dustin's eyes got wider and wider. This girl was nuts! It felt like this tongue vacuum was going to suck his tongue right out of his mouth! "A tongue vacuum?!" Dustin gurgled, barely able to talk.

"Yes!" Quinn chortled gleefully. "I'm sucking the germs off your tongue!" She let the machine run for a few more seconds before turning it off. "There," she said, feeling satisfied. "Let me see it." She reached in and grabbed Dustin's tongue, turning it over in her fingers. She inspected it thoroughly.

"Hmmm . . ." she murmured thoughtfully. "It still looks germy." She gazed at her Quinnvention. "Maybe this thing doesn't suck enough."

Dustin put his hand up to his mouth protectively. If it sucked any more, it *would* suck his tongue right out! "Trust me, it sucks enough," he said solemnly.

In the drama club classroom, auditions continued. Wiped out from listening to people read lines from his play over and over (and over), Chase was glad the tryouts were almost finished.

"And auditioning last is . . . Logan Reese," Mr. Fletcher said.

Chase did a double take as Logan strolled nonchalantly into the classroom.

"Right here," Logan said, raising a hand and waving casually.

What? Chase couldn't believe his ears. He stared, dumbfounded, at Logan, who carried a script and looked like his usual cool self in a black-and-red tank top.

"Uhhh, 'scuse me a sec . . ." Chase got to his feet and hurried to meet his roomie on the stage.

"What are you doing here?" he whispered, hoping this was all just a weird mistake.

Logan shot Chase a look. Wasn't it obvious? "Tryin' out for the play," he said.

Chase was annoyed. First Logan said his play was uncool. Then he teased Michael and Chase for being in it. Now he was showing up to audition? "But you're always sayin' drama club's lame," Chase pointed out.

Logan shrugged. "You changed my mind. You said it rocks." He pointed to Chase with his rolled-up script.

"So?" Chase said.

"So the drama club rocks . . . I rock," he said, stating the obvious. "It should be a good match, right?"

Chase shook his head slowly as he walked back to Mr. Fletcher. This did not look good. Logan was up to something, and Chase suspected it had everything to do with Zoey.

"Okay, Logan," Chase said with resignation. "Go for it."

Logan glanced at his script one last time, then dropped it on the stage behind him. "Zorka, I have a confession to make," Logan said earnestly. "The truth is . . ." He paused, his eyes full of emotion. "I've had more fun with you this past week than I've ever had with any other girl. When you laugh, I laugh. When you cry, I cry. . . ." He dropped his hands to his sides.

Logan was totally wrapped up in declaring his feelings for the alien who had nearly drowned near his beach — or at least, he appeared to be. Inside, he was smirking. He was nailing it! Acting wasn't that hard, really. You just had to pretend you actually *meant* what you said. It was a little like lying, and he was pretty good at that.

Chase stared at his emoting roommate. It was terrible. He was . . . perfect. Handsome, sincere, completely in character. The whole audience, and Mr. Fletcher, looked spellbound. It made Chase want to cheer . . . and throw up.

"I know you're from another galaxy, and I'm just a lifeguard from Earth, but I don't care if we're different." Logan paused for just the right amount of time. "I love you," he finished, lowering his voice.

The drama classroom was completely silent as Logan finished his monologue. Then everyone burst into applause. Everyone except Chase.

"Fabulous, fabulous!" Mr. Fletcher exclaimed, clapping. "Chase, wasn't that fabulous?" he asked without waiting for an answer. "You were *fabulous*!" he shouted toward the stage.

Logan nodded knowingly. He was fabulous.

Mr. Fletcher turned to Chase and looked him in the eye. "Chase," he said seriously, "we have to give this boy the lead," he said under his breath.

"What?" Chase couldn't believe it. Well, okay, he could believe it. Logan was awesome. But he really, really, really didn't want to give him the lead. "You said I should play the lifeguard."

"I know, but you saw his performance. He's a star!" Mr. Fletcher was beaming, like a Hollywood scout who had just discovered the next "it" boy.

Chase felt like he had fallen into quicksand. The more he tried to get out, the more buried he got.

"Look, you want your play to be as good as it can be, right?" Mr. Fletcher said, trying a new angle.

Chase thought for a moment. Of course he did. But Logan . . . in *his* part?!

He looked at Mr. Fletcher's hopeful face. He wanted Logan to play the lifeguard. Logan's audition was flawless. And Mr. Fletcher was the director. . . .

"Okay," Chase finally agreed, feeling miserable. "I guess we should give the part to Logan —"

"Yay!" Mr. Fletcher cheered, cutting Chase off. He leaped to his feet and practically knocked Chase off his seat as he raced onto the stage to Logan.

"Congratulations, Mr. Reese," he said, shaking his hand vigorously. "You are playing the lead!"

Logan shrugged. Of course he was. Who else around here could be as charming and great an actor as he was? Nobody. "Yeah, I figured," he said.

Chase walked up to Logan with his head down. "Congrats, dude. You were great," he said, slapping Logan's hand. He knew it was true, but saying it out loud was supremely tough.

"I know," Logan replied. Didn't everybody? Well, if they didn't, they would on opening night. Logan was going to rock, and everyone could see him in his glory. "And Zoey's playin' the lead girl, right?"

Chase winced. "Yeah, she is," he said. He had never noticed how much Logan looked like a weasel.

"Sweet," Logan said with a nod and a smirk.

"Later, man," he said, giving Chase a low five.

Chase felt sick as he watched Logan go. As the biggest ego on campus disappeared out the door, the quicksand rose up to his neck.

From Bad to Worse

Zoey stared at Chase like he had just told her the world was going to explode. He had, in a way.

"Logan?!" She could not think of a worse person to have to play opposite in the show. He was arrogant, snotty, full of himself, cute. Wait, forget cute. It didn't matter! The guy was a class-A jerk.

"I know!" Chase said, throwing up his hands in agreement. He was totally relieved that Zoey felt the same way he did.

"How did this happen?!" This had to be a nightmare. She could *not* do a play with Logan! She needed to wake up!

"He auditioned and . . ."

Zoey listened intently, but Chase didn't finish. "And . . . ?" she prompted.

Chase sighed. He may as well say it. "He was slightly awesome," he admitted with a shrug.

Zoey had to admit she was surprised to hear this. She'd always thought of actors as being sensitive, artistic types. Logan was about as sensitive as a rock and as artistic as an algebra textbook. She shook her head. "This is horrible," she said.

"I know," Chase agreed.

"I don't even like *talking* to Logan." Zoey's hands were moving fast. "How can I do an entire play with him?"

"I don't see how!" Chase said, feeling better than he had in twenty-four hours. He could feel the quicksand releasing its grip. "'Cause . . . ya know, the lead girl has to kiss him at the end." Chase watched Zoey out of the corner of his eye and held his breath, waiting to hear her reaction.

"Ugh, sick," Zoey said. Having to kiss Logan was just about the grossest thing she could think of.

"That's what I'm sayin'," Chase said enthusiastically.

Zoey was thoughtful for a minute. "You think I should quit?" she asked slowly. She didn't want to hurt Chase's feelings, but she really wasn't sure she could go through with the play if Logan was playing the lead.

"Yes!" Chase exclaimed more happily than he'd meant to. He didn't want Zoey to know the real reason he wanted her to back out. Watching her act with Logan would be torture. He may as well be put on a medieval rack and stretched until his bones cracked.

"I mean," he corrected himself, "I'd be disappointed, but I'd totally understand."

Zoey sighed. She'd really been looking forward to acting in her first play. But given her choices . . . "'Kay, I'll tell Mr. Fletcher I'm out," she said. Totally bummed, she headed off to the drama classroom.

Chase paused to do a little victory dance. He shook his fists in the air. His heart might just make it after all. When his mini-celebration was over, he followed Zoey to class.

In the school auditorium, rehearsal was already under way. Logan was onstage with several other actors rehearsing a scene. Chase led Zoey over to Mr. Fletcher right away. The sooner she told the teacher she was out of the play, the better.

"Remember to enunciate," Mr. Fletcher instructed. "And let's get going."

Chase tapped Mr. Fletcher on the shoulder. "Excuse me, Mr. Fletcher?" he whispered.

Mr. Fletcher waved Chase away like an annoying

bug. “Shhh!” he said. “Action!” he told the actors. His eyes were open wide. He was obviously engrossed in the scene, and Logan in particular.

Onstage, Logan’s character — the lifeguard — was confiding to Michael’s character — a surfer dude. “I know I’ve gone out with a lot of girls, but . . . I dunno . . . Zorka’s different.” He really thought that girls were a dime a dozen, but he was trying to sound convincing. He stared out at the mostly empty rows of seats. “. . . and beautiful . . .”

Zoey leaned forward in her seat. Was this Logan? He was so different . . . so sweet, so sincere. Maybe she had misjudged him. Maybe underneath it all he really was a great guy.

“. . . more so than any other girl I’ve ever known. So beautiful . . . it almost hurts.” He gazed out at the auditorium, his eyes full of pain.

Whoa! Zoey felt her heart thudding in her chest. Logan was an awesome actor. Being onstage with him would not only be bearable, it would be really fun.

“And that’s the scene,” Logan said, breaking out of his love-struck character. The students in the auditorium clapped wildly.

“Goose bumps!” Mr. Fletcher exclaimed gleefully. “Bumps on geese!”

Zoey looked over at Chase. Should she tell him

she'd changed her mind? Maybe she should break it to him slowly. . . . "Wow, he's amazing," she began.

"Yeah," Chase said begrudgingly. Zoey was getting sucked into Logan's performance. He had to act fast to get her officially out of the production. "Uh, Mr. Fletcher, Zoey needs to talk to you about the play . . . right now."

Mr. Fletcher turned to Zoey. "Yes, what is it?" he asked, still glowing from watching Logan's performance.

Zoey hesitated. She looked at Chase. She couldn't quit, not now. This was too great an opportunity to pass up! "When do we start rehearsal?" she asked, totally psyched. She stood up, grabbed a script from a nearby seat, and raced up to the stage.

Chase's jaw dropped as he watched Zoey chat with Logan onstage. He felt like he'd been kicked in the chest. Once again, the quicksand enveloped his neck.

Spellbound

Zoey walked out of rehearsal with her big blue bag slung over one shoulder. It matched the stripes in her blue-and-white capris, which looked awesome with her printed shirt and pink belt. As she rounded the corner of the building, Logan hurried to catch up with her.

"Hey." Logan lifted his chin. His tone was totally casual. "If you wanna run lines later, come by the dorm." He flashed Zoey one of his lazy smiles. The same smile that Zoey used to want to wipe right off his face.

"Cool, thanks." Zoey could hardly believe hanging out with Logan actually *did* sound cool. Two days ago she would have avoided him like the West Nile virus. Then again, two days ago she hadn't seen him act.

Logan gave Zoey a catch-you-later nod as she peeled off to chat with Chase, who was slouching on the edge of a big planter.

"Hey!" Zoey said, grabbing a seat beside the playwright. Chase looked at Logan walking away, then he looked back at Zoey, gazing up through his mane of dark curls. He was not smiling. In fact, he looked kind of disgusted. "What?" Zoey asked.

"I thought you were going to quit the play. What was that?!" Chase was talking fast.

"I don't know . . . when I saw Logan act . . ." Zoey couldn't really explain it to herself. How was she supposed to explain it to Chase? Logan was just . . . different when he was onstage. "I guess I just got . . . swept up."

"Well, sweep down!" Chase blurted.

"Huh?" Zoey gave Chase a baffled look. He wasn't making any sense.

"I don't know!" Chase shrugged. He didn't always make sense when he was upset. And he was upset. But he couldn't exactly tell Zoey right out that he wanted her to quit because the thought of her spending time with Logan made him crazy.

"I thought you wanted me to be in your play. Why are you all upset?" Zoey had seen Chase in some pretty weird moods, but this was a new one.

"I'm not upset," Chase lied. "If I was upset, could I do this?" Chase stuck his tongue out, smiled cheesily, and waggled his fingers in the air like a cross between a circus clown and a wacky salesman.

It was hardly convincing. He still looked upset — upset and crazy, but definitely upset. "Okay." Zoey had seen enough. "When you wanna tell me what's buggin' you, lemme know." She rolled her eyes. She didn't even try to hide the annoyance in her voice as she shouldered her bag and walked away. Why should she? If Chase was upset about something, he should just tell her. What was so hard about that?

Nicole, Dana, and Zoey parked their trays of salads and waters on a big green table outside and sat down. There was something Nicole had been dying to ask Zoey ever since rehearsal, and lunch was the perfect time to do it.

"So, how can you be in a play with Logan?" He had to be the biggest jerk in the school — or at least the biggest jerk to the girls in the school. He was so full of himself it was a wonder he didn't pop.

Zoey had to admit the question didn't really surprise her. Logan *was* a jerk, or at least he used to be. Now he seemed . . . different. "Have you seen him act?" Zoey asked. "He's, like, *incredible*." There was no other word for it. Nicole should have known that, since she was in the play, too. Had she been sleeping through rehearsals?

"Yeah, but —" Dana didn't care what Logan acted like when he was onstage. It was the way he acted when he was offstage that mattered. "He's such a jerk."

"You'd know," Nicole taunted Dana from across the table. Bad move. Dana took aim and fired, and she never missed.

"Ow! She flicked an olive at me," Nicole complained, quickly checking to make sure the olive hadn't left a mark on her pale yellow boatneck T-shirt. She'd just washed it!

Dana lifted her fist in triumph, showing off her black-leather-and-metal motorcycle cuff. It looked great with her sleek black tank top.

Zoey looked from Nicole to Dana and back. Sometimes they were like kids in the backseat on a long drive. But they were also her best friends.

"All right . . ." Zoey wanted them to understand how she felt about Logan. It was time for a little confession. "I know this is going to sound weird, but when he's onstage, it's like . . . I see him as a different person."

"What do you mean?" Nicole looked baffled.

"I don't know. . . ." Zoey shrugged. "He just seems so . . . sincere and sweet."

"Yeah, but it's still Logan." Dana shook her head. She didn't care how sweet he "seemed." A jerk was a jerk, no matter what.

"And in the last scene you have to kiss him," Nicole reminded Zoey, waving her fork in the air.

As if Zoey could forget that little fact. "I know." She tried to blow it off, like it was totally casual.

"Wait . . ." Nicole's big brown eyes were bigger than usual. Her mouth dropped open. "Do you like him?" she asked.

"I didn't say that." Zoey looked down at her salad.

"You didn't *not* say it," Nicole pointed out. She looked at Dana. Dana cocked an eyebrow. They both looked at Zoey, who conveniently made sure her mouth was too full of salad to say anything at all.

The next day at rehearsal, it happened all over again. Zoey kept reminding herself it was just Logan as she took her place onstage. She had been reminding herself it was just Logan from the moment she'd woken up. She reminded herself again now. *It's just Logan. The same guy who tried to cream you on the basketball court. The same guy who* used *to play center*.

"Ready? Ready?" Mr. Fletcher ducked in between

the actors, looking from one to the other. He was as bubbly as ever. "And . . . action," he called as he jumped offstage to watch.

"So, what do you think of Earth so far?" When Logan said his first line, his voice was full of concern. He sounded like he really wanted to know.

"Earth is nice." Zoey smiled into Logan's eyes. She had never noticed how brown they were before — like chocolate. "We don't have beaches like this on my planet."

"We don't have girls like you on my planet." Logan smiled back.

"You mean girls with antennas and weird eyebrows?" Zoey spoke her line without taking her eyes from Logan's face. She couldn't stop looking at him!

"No. I mean girls who aren't afraid to be themselves." Every word coming from Logan's mouth sounded like it had been sent straight from his heart. Zoey was lost in his eyes, waiting for his next word.

"You're amazing," Logan said. It was like he was speaking to her alone. Like they were the only two people in the whole world. Zoey felt hypnotized. She could listen to Logan forever. "You're . . . you're perfect," he finished.

So are you, Zoey thought.

Rewrite

"It's my own fault," Chase complained to Michael on their way to class. It was true. He had created the monster that was terrorizing him. "I mean, why'd I have to write a play in the first place?!"

"'Cause you stink at sports?" Michael asked plainly. That was Michael. Always right there with the honest answer when you *didn't* need it.

"Whatever." Chase blew him off. He was not looking for *funny*, he was looking for *help*. "Now Logan is going to kiss Zoey in the play." Chase moped. "And, the worst part is, she's gonna let him!"

"Didn't they already kiss in rehearsal?" Michael asked, sticking his hand into the pocket of his long denim shorts.

"No. Fletcher wants to save it for the actual performance," Chase explained. He launched into his best

Fletcher imitation. "'To preserve the magic.'" Chase plastered on a fake grin, then let the smile fade. The only magic Chase wanted to see onstage was a big puff of smoke that would make Logan disappear.

"You got it bad for Zoey, doncha?" Michael had always suspected a crush. But the way Chase was acting now clinched it.

"No," Chase said, denying everything. "I just . . . don't think it's proper for a young woman to be kissing in public."

"You didn't care when it was you she was gonna kiss," Michael pointed out.

Chase stopped dead in his tracks. There he went again with the right answer at the wrong moment. "Look, you wanna be Logic Man or you wanna be my friend? I'm dyin' here." Chase could really use a little help.

"All right. Calm down," Michael said, shouldering his orange backpack. If Chase needed help, Michael would give him help. "Let me ask you this. It's your play, right?"

"Yeah. So?" Chase had no idea what his roommate was getting at.

"So, if it's buggin' you that much, go change it."

"Change it?" Chase was liking the sound of this.

"Write a different ending," Michael said. Simple. How was that for Logic Man?

If there had been a lightbulb over Chase's head it would have lit up. "I can get rid of the kiss!" He grinned.

"That's what I'm saying." Michael smiled easily.

Chase turned and faced Michael. He was almost at a loss. "Michael, you, my friend, are a genius in short pants!" Chase pressed his water bottle into Michael's hand like he was giving him an award before racing toward his room and waiting laptop.

Michael accepted the water and humbly took a swig. He had to agree with Chase. "I have my moments," he said to no one in particular.

It was dark out before Chase finally got the chance to make the necessary changes to his play. Lying in bed, dressed in plaid jammie bottoms and a T-shirt, he stared at the glowing screen in front of him. One line leaped out: *Zorka leans in to kiss the lifeguard.*

Zorka leans in to kiss the lifeguard. It played over and over in his head. *Zorka leans in to kiss the lifeguard.* Chase took a swig of water. Then the answer came to him, clear as day. Just two little letters should do the trick. Chase tapped the keys, replacing two little S's with L's. *Zorka leaned in to* kill *the lifeguard.* There. Chase sat back, took another sip of water from his bottle, and smiled. His work here was done.

* * *

Mr. Fletcher stared at the last page of the script. Lowering his reading glasses halfway, he looked again. Horror showed plainly on his face. "Kill?" he cried in disbelief. "Kill?"

Chase grinned and nodded. Yes, kill. It was music to his ears. "Yeah. See, she's really actually supposed to kill the lifeguard. 'Kiss' was just a typo," he explained. Mr. Fletcher shook his head as he arranged the props on the lifeguard stand onstage. "I'm always mixing up my S's and L's," Chase tried to play it off. "Like one time I tried to write sassafras and I wrote lallafral."

"Chase," Mr. Fletcher said, calmly giving him a meaningful look. "The sign of a true writer is to know when to put the pen down and walk away."

"I hear ya, but —"

"I am not going to let you change one word of this play." Mr. Fletcher put his hand on Chase's shoulder. He leaned down and smiled. "It's perfect." He chuckled.

Chase forced himself to smile back at the compliment. Yeah. Just perfect.

Meanwhile Dustin, still sick as a dog, stared at the ceiling in Quinn's room. His head throbbed. He was hot. No, cold. No, hot. And he could not stop coughing. It felt good to lie down. He was glad Quinn suggested it. He just needed to rest. But suddenly Dustin felt a breeze on his feet.

"Why are you taking off my shoes?" he asked between coughing fits.

"I'm going to cure you by applying proton impulses to the soles of your feet," Quinn answered, making sure Dustin's feet were secured in the ankle braces at the end of the bed. Quinn's braids bobbed as she worked.

"Can I please leave?" Dustin's voice was weak. He sounded pathetic. And he had absolutely no idea why he'd come back to see Quinn after the tongue vacuum incident. Maybe he'd been momentarily insane. Or maybe he thought she could actually cure him.

"No," Quinn answered. She was almost ready. She positioned her protective eye goggles. "Ready?"

"No," Dustin protested uselessly.

Aiming her proton device between Dustin's feet, a blue bolt of arcing laser light shot out, forked, and found its twin targets. The light played on the soles of Dustin's feet. Immediately Dustin began to convulse.

"Ahhh! That tickles!" Dustin gasped as his feet flailed in their restraints.

Quinn stopped the proton stream. "Do you feel better?" she asked.

"No," Dustin sighed, catching his breath. Thank goodness that was over.

"I'll adjust the proton saturation." Quinn fiddled with her equipment and fired again. This time the energy streams were green.

"Ahh!" Dustin screamed. And laughed. And coughed. And screamed again. "It's not making me better!" he yelled. He wasn't sure Quinn could even understand him since his body was jerking all over the place and he could not stop laughing *or* coughing.

The beam did not seem to be working. Quinn didn't understand it. There was just one higher level of proton saturation. She adjusted the controls once more and fired. The stream hitting Dustin's feet grew brighter, and the sick boy's protests were drowned out by his hysterical laughter.

Sick of It

Zoey sat back and soaked up a little sun on the benches in the quad between class. She was hanging with Dana and Nicole and Chase — the usual crew. And they were all talking about the play while they tried to catch up on some homework.

"You were great at rehearsal yesterday," Nicole said to Zoey. "It's like you keep getting better and better."

Zoey wished she could take the credit. But there was a reason she was getting better, and it wasn't practice. "Know why?" she asked, slyly folding her arms.

"Why?" Dana asked. She had to hear this.

"Logan," Zoey admitted.

Chase screwed up his face like he'd just bitten into somebody's gym shorts. Gross.

"I swear, he's such a good actor, he makes me better." Zoey shrugged.

"He really is awesome," Nicole admitted. From her spot onstage as the "hula girl" she had watched him say his lines over and over and still wasn't sick of it.

"Yeah, Logan's fantastic," Chase mocked them. His voice dripped sarcasm. "Isn't he fantastic?" he cooed.

Zoey shot him a look. Chase was being kind of harsh. "I just don't see why you have to pick on him all the time." Zoey stood up for her leading man. "Logan's not such a bad guy."

Nicole leaned in to let Dana and Chase in on a big secret. "She's starting to like him."

"Ya think?" Dana let her eyes roll before assuming her usual scowl. Duh. It was pretty obvious Zoey was falling for Logan.

"What?" Chase looked from Nicole to Dana to Zoey. "That, that, that's insane," he stammered. "It's insane, right, Zoey?"

Zoey wasn't sure what to say. "Yeah . . . I mean . . ."

"You mean what?" Chase demanded.

"I don't know." Zoey took a sip of her drink. "Maybe I do like him!"

"Okay." Chase grabbed his books. He had heard enough. Maybe way too much. One thing was for sure. He couldn't take any more. "I gotta go."

"Where are you going?" Zoey asked. They were just having a conversation. What was his deal?

Chase could not get out of there fast enough. "What difference does it make?"

Mistake number one, writing the play. Mistake number two, telling Logan drama club had cute girls. Mistake number three . . .

Chase hit the stairs walking fast, making a list of all the things he had done to make his life miserable.

Coming up right behind him was Dustin. He looked like Chase felt — awful.

"Hey, Chase," Dustin said hoarsely.

"Hey," Chase mumbled. "Why are you sweating?"

"I'm sick," Dustin said.

"Cool," Chase answered without really listening.

"Hey, I hear your play's gonna be awesome," Dustin said, changing the subject. He needed to take his mind off Quinn . . . and her proton ray.

"It was," Chase said glumly. "Till Logan got the lead role and ruined my life."

"I thought you were the star." Dustin was confused. How much time had he spent in Quinn's laboratory, anyway?

“Not anymore.” Chase shrugged. “Now I’m just the understudy.”

“What’s that mean?” Dustin coughed and coughed and coughed into a tissue.

“It means I’m like the substitute, in case Logan quits, or . . .” An idea was forming in Chase’s head — a good, if slightly evil, one. “. . . gets sick.” Chase fixed his stare on Dustin as the kid finally finished coughing. He was pale, feverish, and coughing . . . perfect!

“Why are you lookin’ at me like that?” Dustin asked nervously. It kind of reminded him of Quinn, and made him feel like a guinea pig trapped in those plastic tube mazes. But once again he felt too weak to run.

“Come with me.” Chase took Dustin’s arm and marched him back to the dorm.

With Dustin still in tow, Chase threw open the door to the room he shared with Michael and Logan. Nobody home. Everything was working out perfectly.

Chase pointed to the top bunk. “This is Logan’s bed.” He grabbed a blue pillow off of it. “This is Logan’s pillow.” He pushed the pillow into Dustin’s hand. Dustin still looked confused. “Cough on it,” Chase prompted him. “Go on, germ it all up.”

Chase was not acting normal, even for Chase. "But he'll get sick," Dustin said slowly.

"Yes!" Chase grinned. That was the plan! "Logan gets sick, and I get to be in the play with Zoey."

"This is weird." Dustin was still unsure. He knew Zoey liked Chase, and he knew she didn't like Logan. But coughing on someone's pillow?

Pulling a five-spot out of his pocket, Chase waved the bill in Dustin's face. The kid was always in need of cash. "Is five bucks weird?" he asked.

"Nope." Dustin snatched the bill and started coughing. He hacked all over both sides of the pillow, covering every inch.

"Niiiice." Chase watched, nodding his approval. Finally, things were looking up!

"For an extra buck I'll sneeze on it," Dustin offered.

"Do it." Chase whipped out the extra dollar, sat back, and watched the germs fly.

The alarm clock went off at eight A.M. It was the moment Chase had been waiting for. It was the moment Logan had been waiting for, too. The leading man jumped out of his top bunk, stretched his muscular arms, and adjusted his black tank before shutting off the alarm.

"Rise and shine, boys. It's my big day!" Logan gloated. Tonight could not come soon enough.

In the lower bunk, Chase rolled over. He felt terrible. His head was pounding. He was hot. No, cold. No, hot. He moaned and coughed into his — no! — Logan's pillow!

"Aw, man." Somehow during the night, Logan's pillow had ended up in Chase's bed along with all of Dustin's germs. Chase added another mistake to the long list of things he'd done that were making him miserable.

As showtime neared, Chase was not feeling any better. If he were home, his parents would give him some cold medicine or aspirin or something. But here at PCA all they had was Nurse Krutcher. She was scary. And she was mean. And she hated kids. Cringing, Chase knocked softly on the door of the nurse's office. He felt *that* bad.

There was no answer. Chase pushed the door open. Nurse Krutcher was at her desk dressed in purple scrubs. Her hair was pulled back in a thick French braid and her back was turned. She must not have heard him. Chase tapped her on the shoulder gently.

Nurse Krutcher sat up straight. She screamed like a guy in a kung-fu movie, grabbed a bat, and swung it at Chase. Luckily he ducked in time.

Chase threw his hands up in the air and shrieked. The big, angry nurse was the scariest thing he had seen in his short life.

"What do you want?" Krutcher asked, lowering the bat. She hated to be woken up. She had been dreaming of a world free of kids.

"I'm . . . I'm . . . sick," Chase stammered. Why else would anyone come here? He just needed something to help him make it to the play. "Listen, can you give me some medicine so I can —"

Still frowning, Nurse Krutcher grabbed a thermometer and poked it into Chase's mouth.

"Look, can you please just give me an aspirin or something? I've gotta be somewhere." It was tough to talk around a thermometer. Luckily it beeped and Nurse Krutcher pulled it out.

"One-oh-one. You're not going anywhere." She stepped closer to Chase, forcing him to back up and fall onto the nearby bed. He bounced back like a spring.

"But I gotta get to my play!" Chase protested. That was why he had come! The huge nurse just glared.

"Lie down!" she commanded loudly.

"Okay," Chase yelled back, backing away. There was no way he was going to win in a fight with Krutcher "the crusher" — not with a fever of one-oh-one, anyway. And lying down did feel good.

"Don't move," the nurse said as she rummaged around for her keys. With one last glare she was gone. Chase heard the key turning in the lock. He was trapped. If he didn't feel so sick, he might have been outraged. But his head was pounding. His eyes were watering. Sinking back against the pillow, he let his eyes close.

Suddenly Logan's face appeared before him. He was dressed as the lifeguard and saying his lines. "We don't have girls like you on my planet," he crooned smoothly. "You're . . . perfect."

Zoey was there, too. She looked like a dream in her cute alien makeup. She *was* a dream, but suddenly Chase's dream turned into a nightmare.

"Can I kiss you?" Logan asked.

"Yes," Zoey sighed.

"Noooo!" Chase sat bolt upright. His eyes flew open. He was wide awake and, sick or not, he could not let that happen. No way.

The Show Must NOT Go On

Chase ran to the door. He tried the handle. Locked. He looked around the nurse's office. The window! Racing over to it, Chase pushed it open.

At that very moment he heard a sound that made his heart freeze — a key in the lock!

Nurse Krutcher opened the door just in time to see Chase disappearing out the window. Nobody left her office with a fever. Nobody.

"Hey! Come back here!" she shouted. Crossing the small office in three steps, Krutcher dove out the window, rolled, and scrambled to her feet.

Running at top speed, Krutcher took off after Chase. For a sick kid, he was really moving. He flew across the campus toward the auditorium.

"I don't like kids," she grumbled.

* * *

Inside the auditorium the seats were filled. Practically every single student and teacher at PCA had turned out for the play. Onstage Zoey and Logan were wowing them.

"Thank you for pulling me out of the water." Zoey felt a couple of butterflies in her stomach. Doing the play in front of a live audience was pretty exciting.

Zoey felt the springy antennas bob on her head. Her sparkly purple shirt and circle skirt stood straight out like a tutu or an intergalactic cheerleader's outfit. And the spot between her eyebrows had been done up with glitter so that she really looked like she was from Zorquesia. Logan, as the lifeguard, was wearing board shorts, pooka shells, a whistle, and a fantastic natural tan. Nicole was standing behind them. She looked totally adorable as a hula girl — cute enough to dance on somebody's dashboard.

"Hey, it's my job." Logan spoke his lines flawlessly. "Besides, it's not every day an incredibly cute alien girl washes up on my beach."

Zoey's heart thudded when Logan complimented her . . . um . . . Zorka. "You think I'm incredibly cute?"

"I incredibly do." Logan smiled at Zoey. She really did look cute in her costume. Logan turned his smile on the audience. They were eating it up — loving him. And who could blame them?

Outside the theater, Chase was starting to think his name was a curse. He did not seem to be able to shake "the crusher," and he had to if he wanted to keep Zoey from kissing Logan.

"Get back here!" the nurse screamed as she thundered after him.

Chase skidded to a halt on a grassy hill. He spotted the doors to the auditorium. "Zoey! Don't do it!" he yelled at the top of his lungs — his last words before he hit the ground.

Nurse Krutcher tackled the curly-haired boy, taking him down with a full-body blow. But she had to hand it to the kid, he was wily. At the last moment he squirmed out of her bone-mashing hold, leaving Krutcher with nothing but a pair of sneakers.

Music swelled in Zoey's ears. Logan's performance was so transporting, she was starting to feel like she really *was* from another planet.

"Earth is nice." She motioned to the sandy set around her. "We don't have beaches like this on my planet."

"We don't have girls like you on my planet." Logan looked deep into Zoey's eyes.

Suddenly Zoey heard her own voice in her head. *Maybe I do like him*. It just didn't seem possible, but here she was. And there he was. And there *was* that fluttery feeling in her stomach.

"Zorka, I know we haven't known each other very long, but, here . . ." Logan held out a necklace made of white shells. "I made you this necklace."

Wondering what it would be like to get a real present from the real Logan, Zoey was momentarily distracted. "For me?" She reached out for the string of shells but the necklace slipped out of her hand and landed on the stage behind a prop rock with a thud.

This was not in the script.

"Um . . . I dropped it," Zoey ad-libbed. The fluttering in her stomach turned to a knot.

"Yeah," Logan said tightly. What was she doing? She was totally messing up. "Why don't we get it?" he said through thin lips. If Zoey didn't pull it together, she was going to make him look bad.

Zoey knelt down behind the rock. Logan knelt down beside her. Hidden from the audience, Logan let her have it. "What are you *doing*?" he hissed.

"I'm sorry . . . I dropped it." Zoey looked at Logan. She was too stunned to say anything else.

"Well, quit bein' so lame!" Logan shot Zoey another nasty look. She was going to ruin his moment of glory!

What was his problem, and what happened to the sweet lifeguard? The class-A jerk was back — with a vengeance.

In the back of the theater a coughing kid, wearing no shoes, stumbled in — the playwright himself, still hoping for a rewrite. Chase looked toward the stage. Logan and Zoey were hidden behind the rock. What the heck were they doing back there? Chase tried to catch his breath between coughs.

Onstage the drama was getting real — really real!

"Now be careful! This is my big moment so don't mess it up!" Logan glared at Zoey accusingly.

As if! Zoey watched Logan stand up. All he could think about was *himself*! How she had thought he was cute and sweet was beyond her. He really must be a great actor, because for a few days there, Zoey had believed he was actually human.

"Here's your necklace." Logan handed Zoey the necklace when she finally stood up.

"Thanks," she said flatly, wishing she could throw it back in his face.

"As I was saying . . . you're amazing. You're . . . perfect." Logan tried to recapture the scene.

Zoey wasn't buying. "So are you." Zoey recited her line but her heart wasn't in it.

"Can I kiss you?" Logan asked.

"Aw, no . . ." Chase shook his head. It was like driving by an accident. He didn't want to look, but he couldn't turn away. He held his breath. Zoey hadn't said yes yet. . . .

"C'mon, say your line," Logan leaned in and hissed at Zoey. She was standing there like a dummy just staring at him. "You're making me look bad." Standing back, Logan tried again. "I said, can I kiss you?"

In the audience, Mr. Fletcher was balanced on the very edge of his seat. This was not how things were supposed to go. "Say yes," he whispered.

"No." There was no way Zoey was going to let Logan plant one on her.

"This isn't in the script," Mr. Fletcher whispered nervously to a teacher sitting next to him. Zoey was going off the script! Nobody had any idea what was going to happen next.

"What, um, are you crazy?" Logan asked incredulously. Clearly Zoey had lost her mind.

"Why do you even want to kiss me?" Zoey

improvised. She was mad and she'd decided to run with it. If she was going to mess up Logan's moment, she might as well mess it up good!

"Uh . . ." Logan struggled. "'Cause . . . I think you're really special?"

"Oh, well." Zoey pointed at Nicole, who was staring, round-eyed, at the new play developing in front of her. "I guess you think that little hula girl is special, too, because I know you tried to kiss her!"

"What?!" What in the world was Zoey doing to him? "N-no I didn't."

"Hula girl?" Zoey looked to Nicole.

"Oh." Nicole was momentarily stunned. Then she realized what was happening. "Ummm . . . yes! It's true! That lifeguard did try to kiss me!" Nicole was having fun making up new lines. Being dramatic came easily to her.

Under the dark houselights, the audience sat stunned.

"Things are getting spicy." Mr. Fletcher was delighted with the new turn of events.

"Wait, wait a minute." Logan had to regain control. Suddenly all of the girls onstage were working against him.

"Yeah, I thought I liked you, but guess what, Mr. Lifeguard? I don't now, because you're a jerk and this alien girl doesn't hang out with jerks!" Zoey dropped the necklace at Logan's feet, turned, and started off the stage.

"Where are you going?" Logan asked. The play wasn't over yet, was it?

"Back to Zorquesia. Zorka out!" Zoey gave a stiff wave, turned, and left the stage in the most dramatic exit PCA had ever seen. It was the perfect ending.

"The lights!" Mr. Fletcher hissed. The stage went black, and the audience went crazy. Everyone was clapping and cheering.

"Yeah! Awesome! Way to go, Zoey!" Chase might be sick, but he could not remember when he had felt so good. Zoey had rewritten the ending of his play better than he ever could. The look on Logan's face alone had been priceless. If he could, Chase would have given Zoey a Tony Award. "All right! Yeah!" He pumped the air with his fists, cheering until he was more hoarse than ever.

From the wings, Chase caught a glimpse of the world's cutest alien giving him a wave. Then a hand came down. Nurse Krutcher had him in her clutches. Chase didn't have a chance. Still cheering, he let the nurse drag him away. Krutcher or no Krutcher, this was one happy ending.